'I told you!' cried Mari. 'You did it!'

Fliss stared at the sheet on the notice board. Right at the top – there was her name. *Juliet – Felicity Richards.*

'And look who got Romeo,' said Mari, her finger stabbing the paper. 'Tom Mayerling!'

'I can't believe it,' whispered Fliss. 'I thought . . . I thought Samantha would get it.'

'Well, she didn't,' said Mari triumphantly. 'She got . . .' Her finger travelled down the cast list. 'She got – hang on, there's me! I got the Nurse! Wow!'

'That's brilliant,' said Fliss, her eyes shining. 'We'll be in the same scenes!'

'But hang on a minute . . .' said Mari. 'Samantha's not even on the list . . .'

'I don't understand . . .' said Fliss. 'Isn't Samantha in it?'

'Samantha,' said a voice, 'will be Assistant Director.'

Look out for more

stories coming soon!

Strictly Friends?

Ice Dreams

sweet
he♥rts

Star
Crossed

Jo Cotterill

♥ ♥ ♥ ♥ ♥ ♥ ♥

RED FOX

SWEET HEARTS: STAR CROSSED
A RED FOX BOOK 978 1 849 41205 6

First published in Great Britain by Red Fox Books,
an imprint of Random House Children's Books,
A Random House Group Company

This edition published 2010

3 5 7 9 10 8 6 4 2

The Random House Group Limited supports The Forest Stewardship
Council (FSC®), the leading international forest certification organisation.
Our books carrying the FSC label are printed on FSC® certified paper. FSC is
the only forest certification scheme endorsed by the leading environmental
organisations, including Greenpeace. Our paper procurement policy can be
found at www.randomhouse.co.uk/environment

Red Fox Books are published by Random House Children's Books,
61–63 Uxbridge Road, London W5 5SA

www.**kids**at**random**h**ouse**.co.uk
www.**random**h**ouse**.co.uk

Addresses for companies within The Random House Group Limited
can be found at: www.randomhouse.co.uk/offices.htm

THE RANDOM HOUSE GROUP Limited Reg. No. 954009

A CIP catalogue record for this book is available from the British Library.

Printed and bound by CPI Group
(UK) Ltd, Croydon, CR0 4YY

For Chris W-W, a kind friend

Star Crossed

Chapter One

auditions next week

'The next production,' said Candy, looking around to make sure she had everyone's full attention, 'will be *Romeo and Juliet*.'

There was an audible gasp from the assembled group. Fliss turned to her two friends, her eyes shining. '*Romeo and Juliet!* Wow!'

Some of the members of the Circle Youth Theatre Company didn't look so thrilled, however. 'I hate Shakespeare,' moaned Sean, a tall strapping boy with a shock of red hair. 'All that stupid language. Why couldn't he just use proper English?'

'He did,' said Candy, shooting Sean a look. 'It's not his fault you were born four hundred years too late to appreciate it.'

The rest of the group laughed. Sean blushed, his face going the same colour as his hair.

Candy waved some sheets of paper in the air. 'I'll be holding auditions next week. Anyone who wants a part is welcome to come along but, as usual, my decision is final. And think about what you're taking on. We'll be rehearsing pretty intensively during the summer holidays. If you're cast in the play, there's to be no dropping out halfway through rehearsals.' She glanced at Sean. 'Even if you do think the language is stupid.'

The noise level rose as everyone started to chat and call out questions.

'You should try out for Juliet,' said Mari to Fliss. 'You look just right.'

Felicity 'Fliss' Richards was a petite, elfin-looking brunette, with big eyes bordered by long lashes. By contrast, her friend Mari was solidly built with a round face like the moon and thick blonde hair that never seemed to stay in its ponytail. Fliss blushed at Mari's words. 'It's not just about looks,' she mumbled.

The third friend of their group, Victoria, patted Fliss on the back. 'You know you're easily the best actress in the company.' She sighed. 'Wish I could say the lines like you do. When you act, it sounds like you've just made up the lines yourself. I sound like I'm reading them out of a book.'

Fliss grinned at her friend. Victoria had beautiful dark skin, was tall and slim, with coloured threads woven into her jet-black hair. 'Don't be silly, Vic. You're fine. It's practice, that's all.'

Mari nodded. 'That's true. Fliss is always reading plays and doing speeches. She must know more Shakespeare than anyone.'

Fliss looked embarrassed. 'Oh, not really. I just like the plays. And *Romeo and Juliet* is my favourite. I can't believe Candy's picked that.'

The Circle Youth Theatre Company only ran in school holidays. Candy had started it up a year ago, and now there were over forty members. Fliss knew that most of them had joined because Candy was such a good director. She taught drama at the local college, and she knew how to get the best out of her actors. She was young, too – only in her twenties – so the cast never felt like they were being talked down to. She was enthusiastic and encouraging but she didn't take any messing around in rehearsals. Fliss thought to herself that anyone in the street could have guessed Candy was into theatre. She had pink stripes through her hair and always wore such brightly coloured boots that people turned to stare. Fliss wished she were brave enough to wear something like that!

'I thought she'd go for another musical after *The Little Match Girl* at Easter,' said Mari. 'Glad she didn't though. I hated singing in that.'

'At least you didn't have to play a boy,' said Victoria. 'It was so embarrassing.'

'Seriously, though,' said Mari to Fliss. 'You should definitely go for Juliet.'

'Especially,' said Victoria, 'if Tom Mayerling is going to be Romeo.'

Three pairs of eyes turned to the far side of the room, where a tall boy with curly brown hair and a cheeky grin was laughing with his mates. The three girls sighed in unison.

'He is so far out of our league,' said Mari sadly.

'Too gorgeous for words,' agreed Victoria. 'And hardly knows we exist.'

'I can't believe he's joined the company,' said Mari. 'I never thought we'd get closer than seeing him on the bus to school.'

'Don't suppose we'll get any closer now,' said Victoria with a sigh. 'He'll never notice us.'

Fliss said nothing. She found it hard to joke about Tom. His smile did funny things to her insides. She knew Mari and Victoria fancied him, but it was only in a not-very-serious way. Whereas Fliss sometimes found it hard to sleep at night because all she could see was his face, hear his laugh. He wasn't even at their school and she'd barely spoken to him, but every time she stepped onto the bus, her heart gave a leap when she caught sight of him. When she'd seen him walking into the studio with everyone else, she'd felt as though her stomach had turned completely upside down.

'He has to play Romeo, surely,' said Victoria. 'He's the best looking. And he was brilliant in his school play, somebody said.'

'Mercutio is a better part,' said Fliss, trying not to look at Tom. 'It's got more life. Romeo is a bit of a passive character.'

'Does Mercutio get to snog anyone?' asked Mari.

'No, he dies in a fight.'

'What a waste!' exclaimed Mari. 'No, he should play Romeo and you should play Juliet, Fliss. You'd be the perfect couple.'

Fliss was trying to ignore a tiny crackle of excitement inside her. It wasn't just because of Tom, though. Juliet was such an amazing part. Could she really play Juliet? She was sure she could. It was her dream role! She had read the play over and over again. And if Tom were cast as Romeo, as Mari and Victoria said . . .

Mari interrupted her thoughts. 'There's someone who thinks *she* should play Juliet.' She glared at someone over Fliss's shoulder.

Fliss twisted round to see. Samantha Brooks, a tall

blonde girl with silky hair straight out of a shampoo advert, was throwing back her head and laughing.

'That's a fake laugh,' said Mari.

Victoria agreed. 'You can see it in her eyes. She's laughing to impress someone.'

'Guess who?' said Mari. Tom was watching Samantha from several feet away.

'He wouldn't be taken in by someone like that,' said Victoria uncertainly.

Mari snorted. 'What planet are you on, Victoria? Of course he would! She's gorgeous.'

'Her nose is too pointy,' objected Victoria. 'And she won't do anything that might involve breaking a nail.'

'But she's got confidence oozing out of every exfoliated pore,' said Mari. 'Look at her.'

Fliss looked and felt the crackle of excitement fizzle into nothingness. Samantha was the tallest and most glamorous girl in the company. Only three months ago, she had signed with a model agency, and she delighted in telling anyone who would hear that she had had four jobs already and 'people who know' were saying she had a great career ahead of her.

'Can't act though, can she?' said Victoria maliciously, and Fliss felt a smile creep over her face.

'She goes over the top all the time. Our Fliss is way better than her.'

Mari turned to Fliss. 'You *have* to get that part,' she said urgently. 'I can't play Juliet, I'm too dumpy. And Victoria can't act.'

'Hey!'

'Katie Presley left after *Match Girl*,' Mari went on, ignoring Victoria's outrage. 'She could have done it. But no one else is good enough. Face it, half of the girls here couldn't even remember their lines until the dress rehearsal last time.'

'That's true,' said Victoria. 'Including me.'

'So it has to be you,' Mari said practically. 'We'll help you. Test your lines or something. Anything. But you can't let Samantha play Juliet.'

Victoria's jaw dropped open in horror. 'She would be horrifically awful!'

'And we'd all have to resign,' said Mari. 'I'm not as good as you, Fliss, but I love being in shows. And if you let Samantha beat you at the auditions, I will have to give up the one thing I love most in the world.'

'After chocolate,' said Victoria.

'Yes, after that.'

'And your rabbit.'

'OK, him too.'

'And Robert Pattinson.'

'Shutupshutupshutup. All *right*,' said Mari. 'The thing I love *fourth* best in the world.'

'What about us?' said Victoria.

Mari ignored her. 'You will do it, won't you?' she said to Fliss.

Fliss laughed at the fierceness in her friend's face. 'You are completely mad. I guess I don't have any choice, do I?'

'No, you don't,' said Mari, and grinned.

'Oh, one more thing!' Candy called over the noise. 'Quiet! Listen up! Something I forgot to tell you.' She waited for silence, and then went on, 'The theatre is being refurbished, so we can't use it for the production.'

'What!' Fliss was startled, and immediately disappointed. She loved the little theatre with its fourteen stage lights and tiny dressing rooms.

Candy waved her hand for calm. 'So instead I have decided to present you with a little challenge.' She paused. 'The local council has agreed that *Romeo and Juliet* can be performed outside, in the town park.'

'Outside!' The girls stared at each other.

Suddenly Tom spoke up. 'What if it rains?'

Candy grinned. 'Then you'll get wet, won't you? Don't worry, Tom, we'll have an indoor room as a back-up. So you needn't worry about your hair going flat.'

Tom flushed and ran his hand through his curly hair as his mates chuckled loudly. 'Oh, to be a glove on that hand . . .' murmured Fliss, as she watched him.

Victoria turned, startled. 'What did you say?'

'Huh?' Fliss felt embarrassed. 'Nothing.'

'Yes you did. You said something about being a glove.'

Mari grinned. 'She's quoting the play already, I bet. And too right. You've got to get to work, Fliss! Get that part!'

♥

'I'm home!' Fliss called as she closed the front door.

Her mum, Jeanette, came out from the kitchen, wiping her hands on a tea towel. 'Hello, love. Did you have a nice time?'

'Yeah.' Fliss hung up her jacket and put her keys on the table. 'It was really good to see everyone.' *Especially Tom*, she thought.

'So?' said Jeanette, raising her eyebrows. 'What's the show?'

Fliss took a breath. '*Romeo and Juliet*.'

Jeanette stared. '*Romeo and Juliet?* Why are they doing that then?'

'What do you mean?'

'Well, it's not exactly mainstream, is it?' said Jeanette, draping the tea towel over the sofa and plumping up a cushion. 'Isn't it Shakespeare?'

'Yes.'

'Well, who's going to come and see it? I mean, don't get me wrong, love, but it's a kids' drama club. Don't you think it's a bit – well – ambitious?'

Fliss felt hot. 'I didn't pick it,' she said. 'Candy did.'

Jeanette let out a snort. 'Candy. What kind of a name is that anyway? Is it her stage name?' She said 'stage name' as though it were something to be ashamed of.

'I don't know,' said Fliss, wishing she could just escape upstairs. 'I think it's a nice name.'

Jeanette gave her daughter a pitying look. 'It might be a nice name when you're four years old, but it's not a name for a grown-up, is it? Unless you're an arty sort, I suppose.' She looked at her daughter. 'Oh, don't pull such a long face. I'm sure you'll have lots of fun doing this *Romeo and Juliet* thing. Maybe you'll do a short version. I saw a Shakespeare play once. It went on for hours. I nearly fell asleep. All those old-fashioned words! If Candy has any sense, she'll do it all in modern English so people can actually understand what's going on.'

Fliss wanted to say, 'The language is what makes the play great, don't you see?' but she couldn't. She hated contradicting people even when she disagreed with them.

Jeanette came over to give Fliss a hug. 'I'm sure it'll be a lovely little play. When is it?'

'End of August. But we can't use the theatre so it'll be outside in the park.'

'Well, now I've heard everything,' said Jeanette. 'Acting outside! And what will you do when it rains?'

'Maybe it won't.'

'This is England,' said Jeanette sarcastically. 'It always rains.'

'Candy says there's an indoor venue just in case.' Fliss felt a tiny flicker of annoyance. Why was her mum always so determined to find fault with things?

'Thank goodness for that.' Jeanette picked up the tea towel again and used it to wipe a smudge of flour off her cheek. 'Come into the kitchen with me. I'm making gluten-free cake. Vivienne's coming round tomorrow, and you know what she's like with gluten.'

Fliss nodded, though the news didn't fill her with

pleasure. Her mother's friend Vivienne was obsessed with diet. One week she would say that dairy made you produce more mucus and so she was giving it up to make sure she didn't get colds. The next week she would declare that tomatoes were scientifically proven to prevent cancer and so she was going to eat tomatoes at every meal, even for breakfast. At the moment, Vivienne had decided that wheat and gluten were the cause of her stomach cramps and so she was cutting them out of her diet.

Fliss secretly felt that her mother looked up to Vivienne. Vivienne was smart and intelligent – at least, she said she was – and she was always exclaiming in a surprised voice, 'Oh, didn't you know that? Didn't you hear? I thought everyone knew that nowadays.' Fliss was a little bit afraid of Vivienne. Vivienne made her feel young and stupid. She wondered sometimes if her mother felt like that too.

Jeanette opened the oven door and peered in. 'Good. They look like they do in the recipe book.'

Fliss squinted in after her. 'Are they chocolate? I thought Vivienne didn't eat chocolate?'

'No, no, chocolate's good for you,' said Jeanette, sounding exactly like Vivienne. 'In small amounts, it's been shown to have a beneficial effect on the heart.'

'Oh.'

'It has to be very good quality chocolate, of course,' said Jeanette. She cast a slightly worried look at the wrapper on the counter top. Fliss knew it was a very expensive brand – a long way from Dairy Milk. 'It'll be worth it,' said Jeanette brightly. 'We'll just get cheaper bread this week.'

Fliss said nothing. Money was always tight in their house. Jeanette worked as a receptionist at the town's surgery but it wasn't a high salary and Fliss often came home to find her mother staring at the gas bill or the council tax bill and obsessively doing sums in her accounts book. Fliss felt cross with Vivienne for making her mother worry about money even more.

'Can I help?'

Jeanette smiled at her daughter for the first time since she had got home. 'You can put the kettle on, love. I could murder a cup of tea.'

Fliss carefully emptied out the water that was already in the kettle ('You should always make tea with freshly once-boiled water,' Vivienne had told them) and filled it up again. Her mind was back on the play. 'There are auditions next week,' she said.

'Mmm?' Jeanette was poring over her recipe book again. 'Just checking I've done it all in the right order, you know. I even had to get special flour.'

'Auditions,' said Fliss again. 'For *Romeo and Juliet*.'

Jeanette looked up. 'Why do you need to audition? You're already in the club, aren't you?'

'Company,' corrected Fliss. 'Yes, but this is to see who gets which part.'

Jeanette reached across and patted her hand. 'Try not to worry, love. I'm sure you'll get something, even if it's only a couple of lines. You were quite good in that play at Easter. The one with songs.'

'*The Little Match Girl*,' said Fliss.

'That's the one. You sang your solos very nicely. And I thought you looked lovely in that sweet costume with the bonnet.'

Fliss bit her lip. Hadn't her mother noticed her acting ability as well as her costume? 'Mari says I might get to play Juliet.'

'Who?'

'Mari. You know – my friend.'

'No, not Mari. I know who Mari is. I meant who did she say you could be?'

'Juliet,' said Fliss, as the kettle clicked off. 'The main part.'

There was a pause. 'Aren't you going to pour that out?' said Jeanette. 'Otherwise we'll have to start all over again with new water.'

Hastily, Fliss poured hot water onto the teabag,

squeezed it and dunked it into the second mug. ('Never waste two teabags where one will do,' Vivienne would have admonished. 'Didn't you know there's a world shortage of tea?')

'Well, I think it's really nice that your friends are so supportive,' said Jeanette. 'And I think whatever size of part you get, you should be pleased. After all, it's not like it really matters, is it? It's the taking part that counts.'

'It's not a team sport,' said Fliss in a quiet voice. She added milk to the mugs and put them on the kitchen table. Inside she felt an ache. It was so difficult to talk to her mother about acting. Jeanette didn't seem to understand the first thing about it. How could she explain that she wanted that part more than anything?

'I know it's not a sport,' said Jeanette with a smile. 'But it's basically the same, isn't it? You're in the drama club because it's fun and you get to have fun with other people your own age. Not because you're going to be a great actress someday.'

Fliss curled her fingers around the scalding hot mug. Her heart gave a thump. 'What if I were?' she said, trying to keep her voice light.

'Were what?'

'Going to be a great actress.' Fliss dared to glance up

through her dark lashes at her mother. 'What would you think?'

Jeanette hesitated for a moment, her head on one side and a puzzled expression on her face. Then suddenly she burst out laughing. 'Oh, Felicity! You do know how to wind me up, don't you? Going to be a great actress!' She chuckled again. 'You nearly got me there. I thought you were serious for a moment!'

Fliss gave something that looked like a smile but it didn't reach her eyes. 'Yeah,' she said. 'Just a joke.'

Chapter 2

focus!

'Do I look all right?' Victoria asked for the third time.

Mari made an exasperated noise. 'You look just like you did five minutes ago. Give it a rest, Vic.'

Victoria squirmed on her chair. 'I'm just really nervous, that's all.' All the girls in the Circle Youth Theatre Company were sitting outside the studio that was their main rehearsal space. It was part of the Alexander Arts Centre, a large complex of dance studios and gym halls, and the corridor was long, painted cream, and smelled of socks. Victoria, Fliss and Mari were sitting close to the door, waiting for Candy to come out and call them in one by one. Victoria squirmed again. 'Aren't you nervous?'

'We all are.' Mari glanced to her left. 'You all right, Fliss?'

Fliss was staring into space, her lips moving inaudibly.

'Fliss?'

'Hmm? Oh – yeah, I'm OK. Why wouldn't I be?'

'Aren't you nervous?'

Fliss considered. 'A bit, I suppose. Not properly. Not like nervous before a performance. I mean, it's only Candy in there, isn't it?'

Mari shook her head in wonderment. 'I wish I could be so calm. I know I won't get Juliet, but there's always Lady Capulet, or the Nurse.'

'I won't even be good enough for one of them,' said Victoria gloomily. 'I just hope I don't have to play a boy again.'

Fliss, momentarily diverted, turned to look at her. 'The boys get swords.'

'Ooh,' said Victoria, brightening up. 'That would be fun.'

'You with a sword?' said Mari in horror. 'That wouldn't be fun, it would be a disaster waiting to happen.'

Victoria was about to reply when the door to the studio opened and Candy came out. She looked around at the assembled girls. 'Great to see so many of you,' she said. 'I'll try not to keep you waiting too long, but I have to make sure everyone gets a fair shot, OK?' She frowned. 'Isn't Samantha here?'

Fliss glanced around in surprise. 'Maybe she's not coming,' whispered Mari hopefully.

'I'm sure she'll be along soon,' said Candy. 'I can't imagine she'd want to miss the auditions.'

Mari snorted and then tried to turn it into a cough.

'Mari,' said Candy, 'why don't you come in first? You got a speech sorted?'

'Yum-hum,' mumbled Mari.

'Excellent.' Candy stood aside and held the door open. 'In you come.'

Mari shot a terrified look at Fliss before getting to her feet and shuffling into the studio as though she were walking to her execution.

The door of the studio wasn't soundproof, so before long they could hear Mari's voice rising and falling as she performed her speech, although it wasn't loud enough to hear the words. At one point she faltered, and Fliss held her breath. After a moment, however, Mari resumed, and Fliss and Victoria both breathed a sigh of relief.

'That was the line she always forgets, bet you anything,' whispered Victoria. All three girls had heard each other's speeches so often they knew exactly how it should go. Mari finished her speech and Victoria wriggled on her seat again. 'I hope I'm next,' she said. 'I mean, I don't really because I'm terrified and actually I don't want to go in there at all, but it would be better to get it over and done with, don't you think? Or maybe it'd be better to perform last, when there's no one listening in the corridor. Oh – though the boys might be here by then, I guess. That would be even worse. Doing my speech and knowing . . .'

Fliss let Victoria's voice wash over her. Gazing at the polished linoleum floor, she ran through her speech in her mind again. She had done it so many times now she could have performed it in her sleep. Indeed, only the night before Jeanette had paused outside her daughter's room, puzzled by the low murmuring. Putting her ear to the door, she heard Fliss say, 'In half an hour she promised . . .' Jeanette frowned and pushed open the door, just as Fliss said loudly, 'Oh, she is lame!' Jeanette jumped, but Fliss rubbed her hand across her face, turned over in bed and soon resumed her deep breathing. Jeanette quietly went out of the room and closed the door behind her.

When Mari came out, Victoria went in. Mari was trembling. 'Thank goodness that's over,' she said. 'I need to sit down.'

Fliss couldn't help smiling at the normally

unflappable Mari. 'You're not usually this jumpy.'

'She made me improvise!' said Mari in horror. 'Make stuff up! I can't do that, you know I can't! Give me lines and I know where I am. It was awful. I'll be lucky to get any kind of part after that.'

Fliss squeezed her friend's hand. 'I'm sure you—' she began, but just then there was a commotion at the end of the corridor, and Samantha swept towards them as though blown in by a strong wind.

'God, why can't cyclists stay in their own lanes? That stupid man nearly made me miss the audition!'

'What happened?' asked Eloise, a girl who wished she could be more like Samantha and had even dyed her hair the same shade. 'Sit down and get your breath.'

'I can't sit down,' said Samantha dramatically. 'I'm too wound up. Honestly! They shouldn't even be on the roads – I mean, it's downright dangerous!' Looking round to check that everyone was hanging on her every word, she continued, 'This old man – he must have been at least forty – tried to cycle right across in front of my dad. Wanted to turn down one of the side roads. Dad had to do an emergency stop to make sure he didn't hit him. Don't these cyclists even look behind them?'

'Didn't he put his arm out to show he was turning right?' asked Mari.

Samantha shrugged carelessly. 'Oh, I don't know.'

'That's really dangerous,' said Eloise breathlessly. 'You could have had a really bad accident.'

'I know!' said Samantha. 'That's what I'm saying!'

'But you didn't,' said Mari.

'*Luckily*,' said Eloise, shooting her a look.

'Yeah, because my dad knew what he was doing. Forty miles an hour to zero just like that!' Samantha snapped her fingers. The girls around her nodded, impressed.

'Forty?' asked Mari. 'Where was this?'

'Just down the road,' said Samantha. 'What's that got to do with anything?'

'It's a thirty-mile-an-hour zone,' said Mari. 'Your dad was speeding.'

There was a slight gasp from the watching girls. Samantha's face slowly reddened. Mari stared at her calmly. Fliss screwed up her eyes. She hated confrontation. Mari had never liked Samantha. She thought Samantha was vain and stuck-up and false.

'Some people,' said Samantha in a low hiss, 'should keep their opinions to themselves. Especially when they want a part in this play.'

Mari laughed. 'What are you trying to say? That

you've got some kind of influence over who gets cast?'

Samantha raised one plucked eyebrow. 'I'm just saying Candy doesn't like working with *difficult* people.'

'Yeah,' Eloise butted in. 'And that thirty-mile-an-hour sign is just a guideline anyway.'

There was a slight pause. Eloise looked around. 'What?'

Mari ignored Eloise. 'You think I'm difficult?' she said pointedly to Samantha. 'You have *no* idea how difficult I can be.'

Samantha laughed. 'Is that some kind of ridiculous threat?' She sat down next to Eloise and turned her back on Mari.

Fliss tugged on Mari's hand. 'Mari . . .'

'She's so full of herself!' said Mari in a deliberately loud voice. Some of the other girls started to look annoyed.

'Sit down,' muttered Fliss through gritted teeth.

Mari ignored her. 'She thinks just because she's a model, she's better than anyone else!'

Samantha said to Eloise, 'Some people can't admit they're jealous.'

Eloise nodded wisely. 'Not everyone is as lucky as you.'

'That's right,' said Samantha with a small sigh. She glanced slyly over her shoulder. 'And some people will just never have the figure for modelling.'

Mari pulled her arm out of Fliss's grasp. 'Are you saying I'm fat?' she said furiously.

Samantha rolled her eyes.

'If you've got something to say,' said Mari, her voice getting louder and louder, 'you can say it to my face.'

'I wouldn't dare,' said Samantha smugly, 'if you're really as *difficult* as you say.' Eloise burst into high-pitched giggles.

The door to the studio opened and Candy stuck her head out, frowning. 'What on earth is going on? Can't you even wait quietly out here? How is poor Victoria meant to remember her lines with you lot shouting and cackling in the corridor?'

The girls looked ashamed, though Mari was still trembling with rage. Candy glanced at her. 'Mari, you don't need to hang around now you've finished. Why don't you go outside and get some air? Samantha, good to see you made it.' She swept a stern gaze over them all. 'You should be focused and calm before you perform. If you can't manage that, I shall have to think twice about offering you a part. I don't expect to have to come out here and speak to you again.'

She went back into the studio and the door closed behind her.

Mari turned without another word and walked out. Samantha shook her head and sighed. 'Some people are just too sensitive.' Her eyes had a malicious gleam.

That was nasty, thought Fliss. *Samantha wound Mari up on purpose*. Though, she had to admit, it hadn't taken much doing. Fliss didn't like Samantha either but she didn't have such a personal hatred as Mari. For a moment, Fliss wondered what it was about Samantha that Mari couldn't stand, but there wasn't time to think about that now. *Focus*, Candy had said. *Focus*. Fliss bent her head and closed her eyes, running through the speech yet again in her head.

By the time Victoria came out, the corridor was quiet again. 'I did OK after all,' she said with some relief. 'I didn't mess up my lines too much. I got to the end of the speech anyway. What was going on out here, why was there so much noise?'

Fliss was about to explain, but Candy came out and beckoned to her. 'Come on in, Fliss. I need to keep things moving.'

'Good luck,' said Victoria. 'I'll keep my fingers crossed for you.' She looked at Fliss meaningfully, and Fliss nodded in response. Both Victoria and Mari wanted her to play Juliet, and if Samantha got the part after today's argument with Mari, it seemed likely that Mari would resign as she had promised. Fliss hoped she could convince Candy she was good enough.

'Which speech are you doing for me?' asked Candy, as she settled herself on a chair against the wall.

'Act Two, Scene Five, begins with *The clock struck nine*,' said Fliss.

Candy looked surprised. 'Not the balcony scene?'

Fliss shook her head. 'I thought this had more variety.'

Candy nodded thoughtfully. 'Off you go then.'

Fliss took up her position in the middle of the room, closed her eyes for a moment and concentrated. She was in love . . . she was impatient . . . she was waiting . . . she was in the gardens . . .

Fliss opened her eyes. Around her she no longer saw the bare walls and polished floor of the studio. Instead there was an orchard of fruit trees, their scent carried on the wind. Beneath her feet was soft grass, and to her right was the garden wall, a single gate breaking its length. Fliss's eyes were fixed on this gate. Her whole body tensed with anticipation. 'The clock struck nine when I did send the

Nurse,' she said. 'In half an hour she promised to return.'

Candy watched as Fliss paced the room, exclaiming at the Nurse's lateness, her voice softening as she talked of Romeo and then becoming wittily sarcastic as she commented how 'old folks' behaved as though 'they were dead'.

Almost before she had got into her stride, Fliss discovered the speech was over. Slowly, the room swam back into focus, the smell of the apples disappearing into fantasy.

There was a smattering of applause from the corridor. Victoria must have been listening intently. Candy smiled. 'Very nice, Fliss, thank you.'

Fliss blushed, glad that it had gone as well as in practices.

'How do you see Juliet?' asked Candy. 'What sort of a girl is she?'

Fliss leaned forward eagerly. 'She's young, but she's not stupid. She's been sheltered all her life by her family – she's not really mixed with boys before. So when she meets Romeo, it's like a whole new world opens up for her. She's got so many feelings she doesn't know what to do with them. She's completely unprepared. And because she's quite impulsive, she just goes with her heart.'

'Do you think she should consider her parents' feelings more?' asked Candy.

Fliss shook her head. She felt confident now; Juliet was a character she knew well, almost like a real-life friend. 'She's a teenager in love. Who thinks about their parents at times like that?'

Candy laughed. 'Good point.'

'And I think all the way through she's hoping deep down that she can talk her parents round. If she presents them with Romeo as her husband – they've secretly got married – and says this is the boy I love, she thinks they'll accept him into the family. Because they love her and she's their only child.'

'You sound as though you've thought about this a lot.'

Fliss blushed. 'I've read the play loads of times. It's my favourite.'

'Have you got brothers or sisters?'

'No. I'm an only child. Like Juliet.'

Candy tilted her head to one side. 'And what would your parents say if you decided to get married in secret?'

'I don't have a dad,' said Fliss, 'but my mum would be devastated. She'd probably never speak to me again.'

Candy nodded thoughtfully. 'So you can imagine

how much in love Juliet must be to override her affection for her family.'

Fliss hesitated. 'Yes.' She didn't say she would never do something like that to her mother. No matter how in love she was. The thought of the recriminations, the disappointment in Jeanette's face – they were too much to even imagine.

'Well, thank you very much,' said Candy. 'Would you like to send Eloise in?'

'Don't you want me to improvise?' asked Fliss, surprised.

'No, that's all right. I know what you can do.'

'Oh. Right, then.' Feeling deflated, Fliss went out into the corridor.

Victoria was still there, beaming up at her. 'That sounded brill. You got all the rhythm of the language like you did in practice. Well done!'

'Eloise, she wants you next,' said Fliss. She sat down next to Victoria.

'You weren't in there very long,' said Victoria.

'I know,' said Fliss, rubbing the side of her head. 'I can't work out if that's a good thing or a bad thing. She didn't ask me to improvise like Mari.'

'And me,' said Victoria. 'I was rubbish.'

Fliss frowned. 'You had to improvise too? Why didn't she ask me?'

'Probably thought there wasn't any point,' said Samantha.

Fliss didn't reply. Was Samantha right? Did Candy think she wasn't good enough to improvise?

'I expect there was no point because she saw how amazing you were,' said Victoria in a comforting way. 'We don't have to stay in here. We could go out and see if Mari is still around.'

Fliss cast an anxious look at the studio door. 'I don't know. I just – oh, all right. Let's go outside.'

Mari was lying on her back in the grass. When she saw Fliss and Victoria, she sat up. 'How did it go?'

'Fliss was brilliant as usual,' said Victoria, flopping down beside her. 'I was rubbish.'

'Sorry if I put you off,' said Mari.

'Was that you making all that noise?'

'Yeah.' Mari pulled the head off a daisy. 'That Samantha again. Said I was fat.'

'You're not fat!' said Victoria indignantly. 'She's such an evil moo.'

Fliss said nothing. She didn't want to upset Mari by disagreeing with her. Samantha hadn't *exactly* called her fat . . .

The girls chatted for a while about the auditions, and tried to puzzle out why Fliss hadn't been asked to improvise like the others. In little groups, the other girls gradually came out of the building, some of them settling down on their own patch of grass, others heading off home.

As the girls started to drift away, the boys arrived for their auditions. Mari nudged Fliss. 'There's your Romeo.'

'He's not my Romeo,' said Fliss, blushing as she looked across the grass towards Tom. She wished Mari wasn't quite so jokey about him. But then Fliss found it hard to admit even to her friends how much she liked him.

'He's looking particularly yumptious today,' said Victoria. 'New hair gel?'

'Maybe,' said Mari. 'New T-shirt, definitely.'

'You two,' said Fliss, half-laughing, 'are awful.' But she couldn't stop looking over at Tom. He was deep in conversation with another boy, his forehead creased as he listened. Then he shook his head vigorously and started to argue. Fliss watched as Tom used his hands to illustrate the point he was making. His fingers were long and slender, and his eyes flashed with enthusiasm. Fliss felt as though her stomach were suddenly full of small wriggling things.

'Uh-oh,' said Mari. 'Here comes Samantha.'

Samantha had just emerged from the building,

Eloise tailing her like a small dog. 'You were in there ages,' the girls heard Eloise say.

Samantha glanced around and spotted Tom. Instantly, her voice became slightly raised. 'I was having a long talk with Candy,' she said. 'About Juliet mostly, but also about the play in general.'

'What did you—'

'I have a lot of ideas,' Samantha continued over Eloise's interruption. 'About staging and things like that. A lot of the time, plays like Shakespeare are done without much imagination. I went to see *Hamlet* with school last term and it was really boring. All doom and gloom and black and white. So *depressing*.' Eloise was nodding in agreement.

Victoria looked at Fliss. 'Isn't *Hamlet* the one where loads of people get murdered?'

'Yes.'

Mari nodded towards Samantha. 'She'd probably have the characters in rainbow costumes, stabbing each other to death to the accompaniment of Girls Aloud.'

Fliss giggled.

Samantha was still holding forth, and most of the people within earshot had turned to look at her – including Tom. 'I was saying how the language needs to be kept fresh. Especially if you're going to get kids like us to enjoy it. If people do *Hamlet* like the Royal Shakespeare Company all the time, it's no wonder teenagers don't like Shakespeare.'

A couple of nearby boys laughed. Samantha grinned, enjoying the attention. 'I mean, who actually likes reading Shakespeare at school?'

I do, thought Fliss to herself.

'Not me!' squeaked Eloise.

'So,' said Samantha, smiling at Tom, 'you've got to give people a theatre experience they won't forget. Jazz it up a bit.'

Tom looked amused. 'Jazz up Shakespeare?' he asked. 'You mean with pop songs and all that?'

'Why not?' said Samantha, tossing her shiny hair. 'Why can't Romeo sing "I Can Be Your Hero, Baby"?'

Most people laughed at that. 'I think I'm going to be sick,' said Mari. 'Queen of the False Nails, look at her.'

'And Juliet could do "Dancing Queen",' suggested Tom.

'Exactly!' cried Samantha.

'Actually, that sounds kind of fun,' murmured Victoria. Mari glared at her. 'I mean, it wouldn't *work*, obviously,' Victoria added hastily.

'Candy said my ideas were really interesting,' said

Samantha to the group of listening faces. 'She said it would be really helpful to have someone with my ideas on the team.'

Mari looked horrified. 'She's not serious, is she?'

'On the team?' wondered Victoria. 'What does that mean?'

'And I was also talking,' went on Samantha, 'about how the two leads need real chemistry. I mean, you have to really *believe* that Romeo and Juliet are head-over-heels in love with each other.' She threw a glance at Tom whilst twiddling the ends of her hair. 'It's about real passion. Don't you think, Tom?'

'Whatever you say, Sam,' said Tom, grinning. 'Sounds like you're the director.'

Samantha gave a giggle. 'Well, not *yet*, but maybe in the future . . .' She fluttered her eyelashes. 'You can play my leading man any day.'

Tom gave a mock bow. 'Honoured, I'm sure.'

Fliss felt slightly sick. How could Samantha flirt with Tom like that in front of everyone? Didn't she feel embarrassed about that kind of thing?

'Anyway,' said Samantha, still looking at Tom, 'I told Candy I felt I was absolutely the right person to play Juliet. I think I was born to play the part. Like it's destiny. You know?'

Tom laughed. 'I don't know about destiny. But I do know if I'm not in there soon there won't be any parts left to get.'

'I'm sorry, am I holding you up?' said Samantha. She gave a wide smile and flicked her hair. 'That was all me, me, me, wasn't it?'

Tom shook his head, amused. 'Come on, guys,' he said. 'Let's leave Samantha to her daydreams out here.' He and the other boys headed into the Alexander Arts Centre.

'Break a leg,' called Samantha. 'Saying good luck to someone on the stage is *actually* bad luck.' She threw a look towards Fliss, Mari and Victoria. 'Gotta dash, my dad's picking me up.'

'Make sure you remind him of the speed cameras,' Mari shouted after her. Samantha pretended she hadn't heard.

'Do you really think she's destined to play Juliet?' asked Fliss in a small voice.

'Of course not,' said Victoria. 'Don't be silly. It's just Samantha being Samantha.'

'She's good though,' said Fliss. 'I know you think she's a bit over the top, but she can act. She can say the lines fine. She was quite good every now and then in *Match Girl*.'

There was a short silence. 'Candy wouldn't be taken

in,' said Mari. 'She'd never want someone playing a lead role who couldn't stop directing the play. You heard what she said. She spent most of her audition telling Candy how to direct it!'

'She'd want the best person in the lead role,' said Fliss.

Mari turned to smile at her. 'Then that's you. No question.'

'Mari's right,' said Victoria. 'You nailed that audition speech. You were brilliant.'

Fliss gave a half-laugh. 'You couldn't even hear it properly.'

'I heard enough,' said Victoria loyally.

'Don't worry about Samantha,' said Mari. 'With any luck, she won't get a part at all!'

Chapter 3

you can't eat dreams

'I told you!' cried Mari. 'You did it!'

Fliss stared at the sheet on the notice board. Right at the top – there was her name. *Juliet – Felicity Richards*.

'And look who got Romeo,' said Mari, her finger stabbing the paper. 'Tom Mayerling!'

'I can't believe it,' whispered Fliss. 'I thought . . . I thought Samantha would get it.'

'Well, she didn't,' said Mari triumphantly. 'She got . . .' Her finger travelled down the cast list. 'She got – hang on, there's me! I got the Nurse! Wow!'

'That's brilliant,' said Fliss, her eyes shining. 'We'll be in the same scenes!'

'But hang on a minute . . .' said Mari. 'Samantha's not even on the list.'

'What?' Fliss peered at the list. 'Are you sure?'

Victoria ran into the room. 'The list is up already? Did I get anything?'

'Umm . . . yes!' Mari pointed. 'You're doing the Chorus, with a couple of other people, and . . . extra courtiers, crowd scenes and stuff.'

Victoria looked relieved. 'So I won't have many lines. That's good. I can be an extra, no problem.'

'But I don't understand . . .' said Fliss. 'What about Samantha?'

'Samantha,' said a voice, 'will be Assistant Director.'

The three of them turned to face Samantha standing in the doorway, looking smug. Her faithful follower Eloise was at her heel.

'Assistant Director?' Mari repeated, as though the words tasted nasty in her mouth.

Samantha tossed her hair. 'Candy had a word with me before making her final decision. She said there was a danger that if I played Juliet, my performance might overbalance the play – it was too powerful. But she said since I had so many ideas about the production, maybe I would like to be her assistant instead.'

Fliss found the courage to speak. 'You'd prefer it to playing Juliet?'

Samantha's face fell for a moment, but then she brightened. 'I may not be the star on the stage, but I shall be the power behind it.'

'But you're just *Assistant* Director, right?' said Mari, with emphasis.

'The *only* Assistant Director,' said Samantha.

'Well, congratulations,' said Fliss, giving a weak smile.

'What did you get?' asked Samantha. 'Lady Capulet? Nurse?'

'Don't you know?' asked Mari in a snarky tone. 'Aren't you *Assistant Director*?'

Samantha looked down her nose at Mari. 'Candy made all the casting decisions once she'd given me my job. I thought it best that she . . .' Her eyes travelled over the list, and her eyebrows rose a full inch. '*Juliet*?' She turned to stare at Fliss. '*You're* playing Juliet?'

Fliss nodded, unable to speak.

Samantha opened her mouth to say something, but changed her mind and smiled sweetly. 'I'm sure you'll be just fine. And of course I'll be in all your rehearsals if you need any advice.'

Fliss went white as Samantha walked out. 'She's going to be in my rehearsals!' she said in a strangled whisper. 'Watching me say my lines!'

'Worse than that,' said Mari. 'She's going to have to watch you kiss Tom.'

Fliss's big eyes seemed to double in size. 'I can't!' she said.

'Of course you can,' said Mari. 'You have to.'

Victoria's hand found Fliss's and squeezed it. 'Don't worry,' she said. 'Once you get on that stage, no one can touch you. Once you become Juliet, Samantha won't even exist.'

Fliss smiled gratefully. 'You're right. When I act, I forget who's watching anyway. Hopefully I'll just get used to it.'

'There you go,' said Victoria. 'And if Candy's doing the actual directing, then maybe Samantha won't have much to do.'

Mari glanced at Victoria as though she were about to disagree, but Victoria glared at her. 'That's right,' Mari said. 'And guess what? You've got me in half your scenes too!'

Fliss beamed. 'True.'

'In fact,' continued Mari, 'things couldn't be much better!'

♥

Jeanette stared at her daughter. 'You're – what did you say?'

'I'm playing Juliet,' said Fliss, feeling as though her smile might break her face in two, it was so wide. 'The lead. I'm playing Juliet.'

Jeanette was speechless for a moment. 'Well,' she said at last. 'Well. I didn't expect that. I suppose this will mean a lot of rehearsals.'

'Um . . .' Fliss felt her smile evaporate. 'I guess so. I haven't got a rehearsal schedule yet.' Wasn't her mother pleased for her?

'And do you have a lot of lines?'

'Juliet is in a lot of scenes, yes,' admitted Fliss.

Jeanette sighed. 'So yet again drama club will be occupying most of your brain for the holidays.'

'Is that bad?' asked Fliss hesitantly. 'School's finished for the year. It's not as though . . .'

'But you've been set work from school, haven't you?' asked Jeanette.

'Some,' said Fliss.

'Just make sure,' said Jeanette, 'that this play doesn't overshadow the more important things. You've got exams coming up soon. You should be looking over everything you learned last year. That's what holidays are for. Not for wasting all your time with drama club. You didn't do so well in your last Maths module, did you?'

'No,' said Fliss quietly.

'Well, this is an opportunity to revise it all again, isn't it?' said Jeanette. Her voice softened. 'I'm not saying you can't have fun, Felicity. I think it's great you've got this hobby. It's good for your confidence. Drama is good for public speaking. Vivienne says her daughter Sofie was quite the dramatic star at her school. And look at her now – a successful teacher, on the career ladder. She'll be a head teacher before she's forty, Vivienne's sure of it. Security and stability – that's what you've got to strive for, Felicity. It's important to relax and have fun. But not so much that you forget about hard work.'

Fliss twisted her hands together. 'What about dreams?' she said hopefully.

Jeanette put a hand under her daughter's chin and lifted it so she could look into Fliss's eyes. 'Everyone has dreams,' she said gently. 'And it's good to have a dream. Always strive for more, Felicity. But you can't run a car on dreams. You can't pay a mortgage with dreams. And you can't eat dreams.' She traced the outline of Fliss's cheek. 'You're such a lovely girl, with so much to offer. It's natural that you can only see the things you like at the moment. But when you're grown up you'll realize that other things are more important. Plenty of people do jobs they don't like, just so they can pay the bills. When you've got the security behind you, then you can spend time on your hobbies. Join the local amateur dramatics company. They do plays twice a year – quite good, I hear. Of course, I've never been to any of them. Not my kind of thing.'

'No,' whispered Fliss.

Jeanette smiled suddenly and flicked her on the nose. 'Although I suppose I'm going to have to come and hear my only daughter say complete gibberish in the park in a few weeks, aren't I?'

Fliss tried to smile.

'Go on,' said Jeanette. 'Go and do something in your room for a while. I'm doing some cleaning in here.'

'OK.' Fliss ran up the stairs. Jeanette looked after her for a moment, a worried expression on her face. Then she turned to face the room, said, 'Right,' and set to work.

♥

Fliss sat cross-legged on her bed, a closed copy of *Romeo and Juliet* in her hands. A highlighter pen rested on her leg, but Fliss was staring into space. Her bedroom was small; it was a box-room really, only just big enough for a single bed. A narrow wardrobe was squashed into the gap between the end of the bed and the window. Fliss had tried to make the room look more personal, but it was hard when you didn't have much space. Bunting in pink and purple hung round the tops of the walls – bunting that Fliss had made herself in textiles at school. The stitching was uneven, and some of the triangles weren't attached very firmly, but you couldn't tell unless you looked closely.

The bedding was white with turquoise edging, and Fliss had customized a small bedside table she had found in a skip, painting it white and gluing seashells to its legs. Some of the shells had broken over time, and Fliss wondered every now and then if she should break them all off and start again.

The problem was that nothing really matched. The carpet was green and had been there when they moved in. Jeanette had promised Fliss a new one years ago, but kept making excuses whenever Fliss brought it up. The truth of the matter was that Jeanette cared more about the downstairs décor than the upstairs, because the downstairs was what guests saw. *Not that we have many guests*, Fliss thought to herself. Only Vivienne, and their house would never impress *her* no matter how nice it looked. Vivienne lived in a modern four-bedroom house on the edge of the council estate, though she always denied its location. 'It's on the main road,' she said, ignoring the fact that it faced onto the side road, which led to the estate.

Fliss's gaze fell on a poster on the wall. It was of some pop star she had fancied a year ago. Had she really fancied him though? Or had she just put the poster up because everyone else fancied him and she thought she should too? Surrounding the poster were numerous postcards that she had collected over the years – Stratford, London, Broadway . . . all of them were of theatres or actors. She hadn't seen most of them, of course, but sometimes a friend or relative sent her a postcard they thought she might like. One or two were small versions of theatre posters – *Twelfth Night* and *An Inspector Calls* sat beside postcards of the Winter Garden on Broadway and the Swan Theatre at Stratford. They seemed magical to Fliss; places where the spotlights and the costumes swept away reality.

Fliss leaned forward and tugged at the poster. It didn't fit – she had outgrown all of that now. She didn't care about pop bands and concerts. She only cared about the theatre. The poster tore across the corner, and Fliss frowned in annoyance. She'd have to do a better job peeling it off the wall and she must make sure it didn't leave a mark on the paint. Jeanette would have words if it did – 'You can't have your room re-painted again, Felicity, it was done three years ago. Make sure you look after it. Vivienne says . . .'

Fliss sighed and her gaze fell on the book in her hands. A smile crept across her lips, transforming her face. The almost permanent worried expression was gone, and in its place was a warmth that made Fliss glow from the inside out. Anyone looking at her at that particular moment would have gasped at her prettiness – something they might not have seen only a minute earlier.

Fliss snapped the top off the pen and turned to Act I Scene 3 – her first scene. Carefully, she began to highlight her lines.

Chapter 4

Let me show you how it should be done

'Quiet, everyone!' called Candy. 'We're going to take it from the top again. Just concentrate. It's not as hard as some of you are making it out to be.'

'Yeah, right,' mumbled Sean, who was clasping Fliss's hand so tightly her fingers were starting to ache. 'Nobody told me we would have to do any dancing.'

'We're supposed to be at a party,' said Fliss, trying not to smile. 'They danced.'

'Stupid history stuff,' said Sean. The music started up again, and he promptly stood on Fliss's foot.

'Ow!'

'Sorry.'

Fliss sighed. When they had gathered for this rehearsal of Act I Scene 5, she had had butterflies in her stomach. This was the scene where Juliet first meets Romeo! And they kiss! She had hardly slept the night before from nervousness.

But instead Candy had so far devoted the rehearsal to the group feast scene, which involved a certain amount of dancing in an old-fashioned courtly style. Candy had brought in Corinne, a friend of hers who taught dance, and so for the last forty minutes, all anyone had done was to shuffle around the floor in a vain attempt to be graceful. Fliss was trying not to feel disappointed, but every now and then she glanced over at Tom, and her stomach flipped again.

'Right,' said Corinne. She was immaculately attired in tracksuit bottoms, leotard and legwarmers, but her long hair was escaping from its ponytail due to all the frustrated head-clasping she had done. 'I think that's enough for now.'

'Thank God for that,' muttered Sean. He let go of Fliss's hand and sank to the floor. 'I need a rest.'

'Some of you,' said Corinne, looking around, 'have made really good progress. *Some* of you' – she glared at Sean – 'need to put in a bit more effort. It's you who's going to look stupid on the stage if you can't do it – not me.'

'Thank you so much for coming in,' said Candy. 'I really appreciate it.'

'No problem,' said Corinne. 'I'll pop back in a couple of weeks to tidy it up.'

Sean groaned.

'OK,' said Candy. 'This is what's going to happen next. We're going to do the early bit of the scene between Capulet and his cousin. And then we'll do the middle bit when Tybalt overhears Romeo talking about Juliet and gets angry. Then I'll send all of you away to practise your lines whilst I take Tom and Fliss for the first meeting. Everyone got that?'

'What about me?' asked Mari. 'I'm in that bit too.'

Candy consulted her script. 'So you are. OK, Mari, you stay.'

Samantha stood up and said loudly, 'If Candy doesn't need you in here, then come next door where I'll be taking people through their lines.'

'We don't have to know our lines for ages yet,' objected Sean.

Samantha looked down her nose at him. 'The earlier you know your lines, the better the rehearsals will be.'

By the time they had finished rehearsing the Capulet and Tybalt sections, it was getting late. Fliss looked anxiously at the clock – would Candy call a halt before they got to the most important bit?

'That's looking good,' said Candy to the group. 'Make sure you write your moves into your scripts. I don't want to have to block the scene all over again next time. It's complicated enough as it is.' She glanced at her watch. 'It's getting late but there's still a bit to do, so maybe I should send those of you who aren't in this section home.'

There was a general murmur of approval to this. Candy nodded. 'All right. So everyone except Fliss, Tom and Mari can go. Samantha, you can go too if you like.'

Samantha looked as though she'd bitten on a lemon. 'That's all right, Candy, I'd prefer to stay. So I can write down the blocking. You know.'

'You sure? All right then. Check your rehearsal schedules,' called Candy, raising her voice as the rest of the company started to chatter their way out of the door. 'I'll see some of you tomorrow, same time, same place. And no excuses. There's no school, so be here on time, please.'

When the room was quiet, Candy turned to face Fliss and Tom. 'Right then, you two. Let's get on with it, shall we?'

Tom nodded, though Fliss noticed he was glancing

across at her. 'I – um,' he said. 'I was wondering. You know where it says they kiss?'

'Yes,' said Candy.

'Well, is that – would they do that? Really, in those days? I mean, they'd only just met.'

Candy smiled. 'They're young and in love. People do things that aren't socially expected when they feel strongly. Don't worry, Tom, you'll be fine. We'll take it step by step.'

'Oh, it's not me,' Tom said hastily. 'I just thought, since Fliss and I don't really – um – know each other, it might be hard for her. You know.' He looked apologetically at Fliss.

Fliss felt a blush creeping up her face. She would much rather Tom hadn't said anything at all about the kiss – she was feeling nervous enough about it as it was! 'Oh, I expect it'll be all right,' she croaked.

Candy smiled. 'I'm guessing you two haven't even had a conversation before, right?'

Fliss shook her head. *Not a conversation*, she thought. *But I can remember every single word he's ever said to me on the school bus. Mostly*, 'sorry', 'is this seat taken?' *and* 'did you want to get off?'

'We take the same bus to school,' said Tom. 'Fliss gets off two stops before me.' He grinned suddenly and stuck out his hand. 'Hi, I'm Tom.'

Fliss felt her mouth curve into a smile. 'Hi,' she said, and shook his hand. Her fingers tingled at the contact. 'I'm Fliss.'

Candy looked amused. 'Very nice. And as rehearsals go on, you'll get to know each other a lot better. I know it can be intimidating to play opposite someone you don't know very well. But I chose you both for these parts because you're good at acting. When you're in character, I think you're matched perfectly.'

What about when we're out of character? Fliss couldn't help wondering. *Are we a perfect match then too?* But that thought made her blush even more.

'Let's get on with it,' said Candy. She gestured to Fliss. 'Fliss, you come and stand over here. Now, your father has had parties before, but this time you're a young woman. No one has ever said these kinds of things to you before. You've spent time with boys like your brother Tybalt, but he's always wanting to fight people. This boy isn't like anyone else you've ever met.'

'Right,' said Fliss.

'So when he talks to you,' said Candy, 'you are completely focused on him and what he's saying. You're swept along.'

Fliss nodded.

'And you,' said Candy to Tom. 'You're a romantic at heart.' Tom pulled a face. '*Romeo* is a romantic,' said Candy firmly. 'He falls in love with girls every day. He writes them love poems. He sees a pretty girl on the street and that's it – he's in love. But this girl – she's different. She's pretty, but there's something about her. Maybe it's just something in the air. But you're hooked. You can't stop staring at her. And maybe it's because you shouldn't be here, or maybe it's the wine you've had, but something makes you take risks you wouldn't normally take.'

Tom nodded.

'Can you do this scene without the script?' asked Candy.

'Yes,' said Fliss. She knew every word of this scene off by heart already.

Tom looked less confident. 'I don't think so,' he said.

'All right,' said Candy. 'Well, hopefully you'll learn it as you go along. This scene will be easier without books.' She sat back. 'Let's give it a whirl, shall we? Just do what comes naturally and we'll worry about blocking it later.'

Fliss took a breath. She was dimly aware of Mari sitting quietly in the corner, and Samantha, a scowl on her face, pencil in hand ready to make notes. But gradually they were vanishing into the distance, as the ballroom around her took shape. She opened her eyes, and she was Juliet. Sure of herself in the environment, but noticing a young man coming towards her. She curtsied slightly. He was staring at her – staring with a strange kind of intensity. Then he reached out to touch her on the shoulder. She felt warm suddenly, and her fingers tingled.

'If I profane with my unworthiest hand,' said the boy, 'this holy shrine, the gentle sin is this.' He sneaked a glance at the book in his hand. 'My lips, two blushing pilgrims, ready stand to smooth that rough touch with a tender kiss.'

Juliet blushed as she replied, 'Good pilgrim, you do wrong your hand too much which manerly devotion shows in this; for saints have hands that pilgrims' hands do touch.' She took his hand in her own. 'And palm to palm is holy palmers' kiss.'

The boy put his head on one side and a teasing light came into his eyes. 'Have not saints lips and holy palmers too?'

Juliet laughed. 'Ay, pilgrim, lips that they must use in prayer.'

'O!' said Romeo, his mouth also curving into a smile. 'Then, dear saint, let lips do what hands do; they pray, grant thou, lest faith turn to despair.'

'Saints do not move,' said Juliet, 'though grant for prayers' sake.'

Romeo leaned forward, glanced at his book and said, 'Then move not, while my prayer's effect I take . . .'

Juliet closed her eyes in anticipation . . .

A tinny version of 'Love Machine' suddenly broke out, and Fliss and Tom jumped in shock.

'Oh, God!' cried Candy. 'So sorry, guys, it's my phone. Hang on.' She dug around in her bag, whilst Fliss and Tom stood awkwardly together. 'What a moment for it to ring!' She looked at the screen and frowned. 'Sorry, I think I'll have to take this. It's my sister.' She tapped the keypad and said, 'Hey, what's up?'

Fliss felt as though someone had thrown a bucket of cold water over her. Juliet's world had gone and she was back in the room with Samantha and Mari, who was giving her the thumbs up from the corner. Tom suddenly noticed he was standing very close to Fliss and took a step backwards, giving her a lopsided grin.

Candy's voice changed. 'Oh no, when? Are you sure? OK. You go with her and I'll be there as soon as I can.

If I set off now I can be with you in an hour. Yeah? Tell her not to worry.'

She hung up and looked at the others. 'I'm so sorry. My mum has fallen over and my sister thinks she's broken her hip. I need to get to the hospital.'

'Don't worry about a thing,' said Samantha, standing up. 'You get going.'

Candy made a helpless gesture to Fliss and Tom. 'I'm so sorry, guys. I thought that was looking really promising. We'll have to work on it another time.'

'No, no,' said Samantha. 'That's why you have an assistant director. For times like this.'

'Samantha, that's very kind of you, but I don't think . . .'

Samantha pushed her hair back. 'Don't be silly, Candy. I'll rehearse it for you. At the very least, we can get through the blocking.' She saw Candy hesitate. 'And if you don't like it, you can just change it next time. What's the harm?'

Every cell in Fliss was screaming: *No, not Samantha! Don't put her in charge!* By the look on Mari's face, Fliss could tell she felt the same.

'Guys?' said Candy. 'Fliss? Tom? Are you happy with that?'

Tom shrugged. 'Sure.'

Fliss nodded helplessly, ignoring Mari's frantic head-shaking. What could she do?

'All right,' said Candy. 'But just play it straight, Samantha. Nothing fancy. This is a simple scene. The words should shine through.'

'Of course,' nodded Samantha. 'Don't worry about a thing.'

The door banged behind Candy, and Samantha turned to look at Fliss. 'Right,' she said, picking up her script. 'Let me show you how it *should* be done.' She walked over to Tom. 'Take a seat, Fliss,' she said. 'Watch me for a bit.'

'Uh . . .' said Fliss.

'Go on.'

Fliss went meekly to sit beside Mari, who turned on her in astonishment. 'What are you doing?'

Fliss shrugged.

'Sam . . .' said Tom. 'Maybe Fliss should . . .'

'Off we go then!' said Samantha brightly. 'From "If I profane", Tom. Now watch, Fliss. Watch how I use the space.'

They began the scene, and Fliss and Mari stared as Samantha flounced around the stage, tossing her hair during Juliet's speeches and flirting out-rageously with Tom. When she said, 'Ay, pilgrim, lips that they must use in prayer,' she leaned

forward and put her finger on his mouth. Tom
looked taken aback. And before he had even got
to the end of the line, 'Then move not', Samantha
had grabbed him by the shoulders and kissed him
full on the lips.

Fliss looked away. Mari's mouth dropped open.
'What is she doing? That's not how Juliet would do
it at all!'

Samantha pulled out of the kiss looking extremely
pleased with herself. 'No interruptions, if you *don't*
mind,' she told Mari. 'Never interrupt the actors.'

Tom looked a bit dazed, but not, Fliss was dis-
apointed to see, in any way unhappy. Samantha turned
back to him. 'Where were we?'

'Uh . . .'

'Your line,' she prompted.

'I can't watch this,' said Mari, and got up. 'Come on,
Fliss.'

Fliss felt all twisted up inside. 'I can't.'

'This isn't a rehearsal,' said Mari. 'It's a disaster.'

Samantha shot her an evil look. 'If you can't
watch quietly then you'd better go,' she said. 'I'm just
demonstrating to Fliss.'

'Yeah, demonstrating how not to act,' said Mari.

Samantha narrowed her eyes. 'You said you were
leaving?'

'Yes,' said Mari. 'Come on, Fliss. Leave Samantha to her private snogging session.'

Fliss glanced at Tom, who was looking bewildered at Mari's outburst. She couldn't just walk out of the rehearsal, could she? What would Candy say? 'You go,' she told Mari. 'I'll be along soon.'

'Fine,' said Mari. 'If you want to watch the Samantha Ego Show, it's up to you.' She picked up her bag and walked out.

Tom gave Fliss a look. 'You OK?' he asked.

But Samantha didn't wait for Fliss to reply. 'Right,' she said, 'now before I was so rudely interrupted, I was trying to make a point. Your Juliet is too timid, Fliss. You've got to make the scene your own.'

'But Juliet is only thirteen,' muttered Fliss. 'And she's never been in love before.'

'But look at what she says,' said Samantha. 'She's flirting with Romeo. She's got to capture his heart.'

'He's already in love with her,' objected Fliss.

Samantha put her hands on her hips. 'Am I the Assistant Director or are you?'

Fliss bit her lip.

'Kiss me again,' Samantha told Tom.

'Huh?' Tom blinked and then grinned. 'You like giving orders, don't you?'

Samantha leaned forward. With her willowy height she was exactly on the same level as Tom. She kissed him gently on the lips. Tom's eyes closed. Fliss felt a kind of ache around her heart. 'You kiss by the book,' whispered Samantha, and giggled. Then she turned to Fliss. 'See? It's all a game.'

'A game,' repeated Fliss miserably.

'I think you should let Fliss do it now,' said Tom suddenly.

'What?' Samantha looked taken aback.

'She's been watching long enough,' said Tom. 'You've got to let her have a go.'

Samantha laughed. 'Well, of course I was going to let her have a go. You didn't think I was going to keep you all to myself all evening, did you? Though if you kiss like that, I'm not sure I can hand you over.' She giggled again, and for a moment Fliss felt dizzy. It was as though there were two Samanthas – the real one and the Juliet one – merging and blurring in front of her.

'Come on then,' said Samantha. 'Unless you want me to show you once more.'

Fliss got hastily to her feet. Samantha laughed again. 'See how anxious she is to kiss you, Tom.'

Tom rolled his eyes, but he looked amused.

Fliss took Samantha's place and they started

the scene again. But every time Fliss said a line, Samantha interrupted. 'No, don't say it like that, Fliss. It's got to have more meaning. Remember what Candy said – the lines have to shine through.' She changed the blocking too. 'Move around a bit more. It's too static. Boring to watch.'

By the time they reached the kiss, Fliss was ready to scream with frustration. Tom was looking more and more annoyed too. When Samantha interrupted just as Tom's lips met Fliss's, he suddenly snapped, 'Can't you just let us get on with it?'

Samantha looked taken aback. 'I was only going to say . . .'

'Well don't,' said Tom shortly. 'I know you're trying to help, but it's getting late. Fliss *can* act, you know. That's why Candy gave her the part. Let her get on with it.'

Samantha's expression dropped. She scowled. 'Fine. Whatever you say.'

Tom turned back to Fliss. 'You OK?'

She smiled, grateful for his help. 'I'm OK. Shall we do it again?'

'Yes. This time with no stopping.' He glanced at the clock on the wall. 'We haven't got much time left.'

They began the scene, and Tom barely looked

at his script. Fliss felt uncomfortable. She felt instinctively that Juliet shouldn't move around too much, but she was aware that Samantha was watching closely, so she tried to incorporate some of the things she wanted. She was relieved when Tom grabbed her arms on 'Then move not, while my prayer's effect I take.' *Here it comes*, she thought suddenly. *Here comes the kiss*. Tom leaned forward, and Fliss closed her eyes obediently.

As Tom's lips met hers, a flash of something like pain shot through her. No – not pain exactly, but so intensely wonderful that it almost hurt.

Tom pulled away. 'Thus from my lips, by thine my sin is purged.'

'Uh . . .' said Fliss, struggling to remember her line. 'Then – then have my lips the sin that they have took.'

'Sin from my lips?' said Tom. 'O trespass sweetly urged!' He pulled her close again. 'Give me my sin again.'

This kiss was even better than the last one. But all too soon it was over. Tom pulled away, looking into her eyes. Fliss stared back. Tom raised his eyebrows. Then he nodded slightly.

'Hmm?' Fliss was puzzled.

'Your line,' he said.

'Oh!' Fliss felt as though she had landed too heavily on the ground. 'Sorry – of course.'

Samantha sighed impatiently. 'Never mind about the line. That was a bit better, I suppose.'

Tom squeezed her hand and then stepped easily away from Fliss. 'I think we should call it a night. I've got to get home.'

Samantha hesitated for a moment, seemingly torn between trying to rehearse more and doing what Tom wanted. 'Yes,' she said, starting to gather up her script and bag. 'It is kind of late. You walking home?'

'Yeah.'

'I'll come with you. It's sort of on my way.'

Tom headed to the door, Samantha chatting away to him. Fliss stood in the middle of the floor. What had just happened? She'd had her first kiss – her very first kiss – with the boy she thought about every day. It had been wonderful; amazing. But Tom was walking off, with Samantha of all people! Samantha had thrown herself at him, and their kiss had certainly looked genuine, but when Tom had kissed Fliss, there had been a connection there, she was sure of it. Maybe he hadn't felt it? Did it mean nothing to him?

Or, worse, had Samantha been a better kisser than she was? Fliss stood miserably in the middle of the floor as her mind whirled and her knees trembled.

Samantha looked back from the doorway. 'Can you switch the lights off when you go, Fliss? Ta!'

The door swung closed behind them.

Chapter 5

she's lying!

'You should complain,' said Mari. 'Tell Candy. I've half a mind to do it myself.'

'But tell her what?' said Fliss. 'Samantha was just doing her job.'

'Sounds like she wasn't just doing her job but doing yours as well,' said Victoria. 'She had no right to make you watch her like that.'

Fliss sighed. 'I know. But it must be hard for her. She really wanted to play Juliet.'

The three girls were lying on the grass of Victoria's back garden. Victoria's mother worked for a big PR firm and her father was a doctor. Victoria's house was easily the nicest out of the three girls'. Her parents even employed a gardener once a week to mow the lawn and weed the flower-beds. Mari and Fliss always came over whenever they could. Fliss's back garden consisted of a small patch of grass and some broken paving slabs. Mari didn't even have a garden, just a paved patio for a barbecue.

Fliss looked up at the sky and watched a bird circling high above her. 'I feel a bit sorry for her in a way,' she said. 'She's so in-your-face all the time. Don't you think that means she must be unhappy?'

'Attention-seeking,' said Mari firmly. 'Shouldn't be allowed to get away with it.'

'I'm surprised,' mused Victoria, 'that Tom didn't say anything.'

'Very weak of him,' said Mari. 'He should have told her where to go – grabbing him and snogging him like that!'

'Seems odd that he didn't stand up to her,' said Victoria.

Mari nodded. 'He's gone down in my estimation since that. I thought he should have stood up for Fliss more.'

Fliss felt hot with embarrassment. 'He did. I mean, he tried to. He told Samantha it was my turn and she should let me have a go.' She picked at the lawn in a dispirited way. 'It was my fault she got away with it all. I should have said something.'

'Yes, but we all know what you're like,' said Mari affectionately. 'Wouldn't say boo to a goose.'

'Do you think he fancies her?' said Victoria suddenly.

Mari stretched out in the sun. 'He's thicker than I thought if he does.'

'She is very pretty,' said Victoria.

'As long as she doesn't open her mouth,' said Mari. 'And she definitely wants him, doesn't she? I mean, all that stuff last night. And walking home with him – she doesn't even live in the same direction!' She turned her head to look at Fliss. 'You OK?'

Fliss nodded miserably.

'If you'd just stand up for yourself a bit more,' said Mari, 'you wouldn't get walked over like that.'

'I do try,' whispered Fliss.

Victoria reached for her hand. 'Leave her alone,' she told Mari. 'Just because you don't mind shooting your mouth off doesn't mean other people can do it.'

'I don't shoot my mouth off,' said Mari. 'I just say what I think.'

'And sometimes that's a really good thing,' said Victoria. 'But we're not all as confident as you.'

Mari sighed. 'I know. Sorry, Fliss. I don't mean to upset you. I just don't like seeing Samantha get one up on you. You're loads better than she is. If she'd played Juliet it would have been awful.'

'Candy said her performance was very powerful,' said Fliss.

'I'll bet it was,' said Mari with a snort. 'Have you seen her do Shakespeare? I saw her do a speech from *A Midsummer Night's Dream* once. She announces every single word, like she's in the Royal Shakespeare Company or something. And she stops at the end of each line! Even if the sentence runs on to the next one! Look, I'll show you.' She jumped to her feet. Fliss and Victoria sat up and watched Mari strike a dramatic pose. 'Wilt thou be gone? It is not yet near day!' She took a deep breath and walked three steps. 'It was the nightingale and not the lark!' She took another breath and turned to face a different direction. 'That pierced the fearful hollow of thine ear!' Her arm shot out in a dramatic gesture. 'Nightly she sings on yon pomegranate tree!'

'Stop, stop,' said Victoria, giggling so hard she could hardly sit upright.

'That's so over the top,' laughed Fliss, trying to catch her breath.

'That's what she's like!' said Mari. 'Can you imagine?' She knelt down in front of Fliss. 'You are the best person to play Juliet, and don't you forget it. Don't let Smarmy Samantha make you think anything different. She's rubbish, she doesn't know anything.'

She took Fliss's hand. 'And I swear I won't have a go at you about being all meek and timid any more, but I shall support you all the way to the bitter end!'

'Hear hear,' said Victoria. Mari took hold of her hand and placed it on top of Fliss's with her own.

'We solemnly swear,' she said, 'to be your bestest friends and to help you out all the way.' She nudged Victoria.

'Oh right,' said Victoria. She put on a deep voice. 'I swear.'

'You two,' said Fliss, 'are the silliest people I ever met. What would I do without you?'

♥

'I'm sorry to call you in for an extra rehearsal,' said Candy to Tom and Fliss. 'I know you worked on this scene the other day with Samantha. But I'm really keen to see what you've done and make sure that you're happy with it too.'

Fliss nodded. She was relieved that Candy was going to take this rehearsal – Victoria had told her that Candy had been away for a couple of days visiting her mother. Samantha had taken a Chorus rehearsal in her absence. 'It was a disaster,' said Victoria. 'Samantha just looked bored through the whole thing, and when we asked her if we were doing it right, she just shrugged and said, "whatever". And then when Simone forgot one of her lines, Samantha went ballistic. Said she had the script in front of her the whole time, how could she forget it was her turn to speak?' Victoria bit her nail. 'It's a good thing Candy's not away for long. I'd resign if Samantha was in charge. Simone said she felt the same way.'

Candy smiled at Tom and Fliss. 'Did it go OK the other day? I know it's a bit embarrassing when you have to kiss someone on stage.'

Fliss blushed and looked at her feet. 'Oh, it was all right,' said Tom. *Just all right?* wondered Fliss.

The door opened suddenly and in came Samantha. 'Sorry I'm late,' she said breathlessly. 'I only just got your message about the extra rehearsal.'

'That's OK,' said Candy, 'but you didn't have to come, you know. I did say you could skip this one.'

'I know,' said Samantha, sitting down and taking out her script and pencil. 'But you know how much I love this play! I couldn't miss a single rehearsal!'

Fliss's heart sank. She had hoped that Samantha wouldn't be present.

'All right,' said Candy. 'Let's get going.'

Tom glanced at Fliss. 'You ready?' he said.

She nodded and took a breath. 'If I profane . . .' began Tom.

At the end of the scene, Fliss and Tom looked at Candy. She was wearing a confused expression. 'Well,' she said hesitantly, 'I can see you've done some thinking about it all. And there are some nice moments.' She rubbed her nose. 'But there's something uncomfortable about it. Fliss – are you – I mean, do you feel the need to move around that much? It's just that it seems to impact on the intensity of the meeting if you're walking around all the time.'

'I think she should try keeping still,' said Samantha. 'I told her in the earlier rehearsal. It'd make for a stronger focus.'

Candy nodded. 'I agree.'

Fliss's jaw dropped. She had been acting the way Samantha had told her to! *I wanted to keep still from the start*, she was bursting to say. *But she told me to be flirty, to move around. It wasn't my choice! Samantha told me to do it like that! She's lying!*

Candy was looking at her. 'Fliss? You happy to try that?'

Fliss nodded, trying to ignore the ball of hurt injustice inside her. Tom opened his mouth as if to say something, but then closed it again, throwing Fliss a puzzled look.

They did the scene again and this time Fliss trusted her own instincts. 'Much better,' said Candy, sounding pleased. 'But Fliss, I think you need to relax a bit more. You don't look very happy yet – Juliet has to be kind of carried away by her feelings. You still look as though you're holding back.'

Fliss nodded. Of course she was holding back! Samantha was glaring at her the whole time!

'Maybe Fliss is just finding her feet,' said Tom.

Fliss looked at him, startled.

'She's naturally quite a quiet person, isn't she?' he went on, and then turned to her. 'Sorry, I mean – you are, aren't you? A bit shy in real life?'

Tongue-tied, she nodded.

Candy smiled. 'Sorry, Fliss. I know it's not easy for you to just let go on stage. But I believe you can do it. You did it in the audition. You have to pretend there's no one watching.'

Fliss's eyes darted automatically to Samantha, who was nodding in agreement. 'Sing like no one's listening, love like you've never been hurt, dance like no one's watching and live like it's heaven on earth,' she said dramatically.

'That's beautiful,' said Candy. 'Dance like no one's watching. Perfect. Can you do that, Fliss?'

Fliss felt trapped. Why couldn't they see? It

was Samantha making her tense up – it was her bare-faced lying – that was what was ruining her acting. To her sudden shock, Tom took her hand. 'Fliss,' he said gently. 'Fliss, it'll be fine.'

She looked up, and her eyes met his. That strange floating yet drowning feeling swept over her as it always did. Tom's eyes were soft. 'Imagine it's just us, right? Just you and me. You can do that, can't you?'

She nodded. He smiled. 'Cool.'

A strange feeling of unreality crept over Fliss. The walls evaporated; she felt carpet under her feet; music in her ears. Romeo approached her. He was the most beautiful thing she had ever seen, and he was so clever with words! She couldn't take her eyes off him. When he kissed her, she felt swept away. It was hard to remember how to speak . . .

When the scene was finished, Candy breathed out. 'That was brilliant, guys. Wow. Do it just like that and I can die happy.' She shook her head. 'Fliss, I don't know what you told yourself, but don't lose it. What you just did – what you just produced – that's the reason I gave you the part.' She laughed. 'In fact, Tom, she just acted you off the stage. You're going to have to raise your game if she's that good.'

Tom grinned. 'I know. Not sure I can keep up.'

Fliss, embarrassed with the praise, snatched a quick

glance at Samantha. Samantha looked as though she was about to be sick, and a warmth spread through Fliss. She had done it! She had proved she was worthy of the part – and she had shown Samantha that she wouldn't be put off by her petty jealousy any more.

'That was impressive,' Tom told Fliss. 'Your eyes do this thing where they go enormous – how do you do that?'

She shrugged. 'I don't know. Maybe it's when I become someone else.'

Samantha made a noise that sounded like, 'Tchuh!' and then pretended it was a sneeze.

'You really do, don't you?' said Tom. 'You weren't Fliss any more. You were Juliet.' He was staring at her. 'You even looked different.'

Candy was nodding. 'She absorbs herself into the part. You have real talent, Fliss. I hardly need to direct you at all. Trust your instincts, you're usually right.'

Samantha started to pack away noisily. 'Are we finished, Candy? Only I've got some stuff to be getting on with.'

The tiniest hint of irritation flashed into Candy's eyes. 'Yes, I think we're done here. Unless you two want to do the scene again?' She looked from one to the other. 'You don't need to from my point of view. As long as you can remember what moves you made, and try to do the same thing next time.'

Tom nodded. 'Sure.'

'OK,' said Candy.

Samantha was already standing by the door, her foot tapping. 'Tom, you coming?'

Tom looked momentarily startled. 'Huh?'

Samantha rolled her eyes. 'You said you'd help me with that audition speech, remember?'

'Audition speech?' repeated Fliss.

Samantha turned to stare at her. 'It's for a production at the Playhouse this Christmas. Oh, didn't you know? It's too late to apply now, I'm afraid. They're only holding auditions this week.'

'Oh, right,' said Fliss. She felt very young suddenly. Here was Samantha going off to auditions and it hadn't even occurred to Fliss that you could do that. And how had she heard about it anyway?

'They're doing *A Christmas Carol*,' Candy said to Fliss. 'They need some street urchins.'

Fliss tried not to smile. She found it hard to imagine Samantha as a street urchin. It seemed far too dirty and unglamorous a role for her!

'You said you'd go through my lines with me,'

Samantha persisted. 'When we were talking yesterday?'

'Oh, right,' said Tom. 'Did I? Yeah, I guess so.'

Fliss packed her script in her bag so that no one could see how upset she was. When had Samantha seen Tom yesterday? There hadn't been a rehearsal. Were they going out? No one had told her they were dating – *but then I'm invisible, aren't I?* she thought to herself. *Off-stage, I'm just timid little Fliss who wouldn't say boo to a goose.*

Samantha said impatiently, 'Come on then, Tom. If you're coming.'

'Yeah,' said Tom. He shot a curious glance at Fliss, but she didn't notice. 'OK.'

When the door had banged behind Samantha and Tom, Candy turned to Fliss. She hesitated. 'Is everything OK, Fliss?'

'What do you mean?'

Candy shook her head. 'I don't know. You tell me. When I auditioned you – and just now, in the scene – you were brilliant. You really get lost in the part. You become Juliet. But sometimes, like earlier – I don't know, it's as though I'm watching a different person. You seem much less sure of yourself, almost awkward. Is there something putting you off?'

Fliss flushed. 'No.'

Candy looked at her closely. 'Is it Tom?'

'No!'

Candy laughed. 'Right. OK, it's not Tom. Is it Samantha, by any chance?'

Fliss looked down at her shoes.

'I know it must be a bit difficult for you,' said Candy. 'Samantha wanting to play Juliet, and all that. But she's got lots of good ideas. I wouldn't have asked her to be assistant director if I didn't think she could do it. Give her a chance.'

Fliss nodded. *I did*, she thought to herself. *I did give her a chance. And look what happened! She told me to act a certain way and then lied about it!*

'OK, Fliss?' said Candy.

'OK,' said Fliss.

Chapter 6

that's what mothers are for

'You're very quiet this evening,' said Jeanette as they sat on the sofa watching the TV. 'Even quieter than usual, I mean.'

'I'm OK,' said Fliss. She took a spoonful of pasta from the bowl on her lap. 'Just a bit tired, that's all.'

'It's all this rehearsing,' said Jeanette, her eyes flicking back to the TV. 'That's what happens when you get a main part. I should have a word with that Candy woman.'

'No!' Fliss looked up, alarmed. 'No, don't. Everything's fine – I'll get an early night. Maybe it's too much sun. It's not the rehearsals.'

'I suppose you're having to do all sorts of lovey-dovey stuff on stage,' said Jeanette. 'Who's that boy again? The one playing Romeo?'

'Tom Mayerling.' Fliss tried to ignore the tiny pang she got when she said his name.

'Tom Mayerling,' repeated Jeanette. 'Is he new?'

'Yes. Just joined.'

'What's he like?' asked Jeanette.

Fliss shrugged, trying to keep her voice casual. 'He's all right.'

Jeanette laughed. 'Nice try, Fliss. You've gone beetroot. Even if you were a better liar your face would give you away. Got a bit of a crush on him, have you?' Fliss bit her lip. Jeanette softened. 'It's all right, sweetheart. You are allowed to fancy boys, you know. It's part of growing up. Just as long as fancying is all you do.' She looked serious for a moment. 'You're so quiet, Felicity. I never know what you're thinking – or even what you're doing, I suppose.' She leaned forward for the remote control and switched off the TV. Then she twisted in her chair to face her daughter. 'You do know you can talk to me, don't you?'

'Mum . . .'

'I mean about boys and things like that. I know you probably think I'm old and have forgotten what it's like.' Jeanette's voice wobbled for a moment and she cleared her throat. 'I'm only thirty-four. And I can remember what it's like to be a teenager in love. Me and your dad . . . well, it was a long time ago now, but I fell in love with him when I was about your age, I suppose.'

Fliss put down her spoon. 'You never said you were that young.'

Jeanette shrugged. 'Not much to say. Not after him walking out like that. But we were together for a long time when I was young. Well, we were both young. I thought we'd be together for ever. You do when you're a teenager in love. I wanted to get a tattoo to prove it would be for ever, but I was too young. Just as well now, eh?'

'What happened?' asked Fliss. Her mother so rarely mentioned her father. Whenever Fliss brought him up, Jeanette would change the subject.

'You know what happened. I got pregnant, he ran away.'

'Yes,' said Fliss, 'but you never really talk about it. What was he like?'

Jeanette looked down at her hands. 'What was he like? Goodness, I don't even know if I can remember now.'

Fliss was sure this was a lie, but she merely said, 'Anything. Any little thing.' *Anything*, she thought, *so that I can better imagine him in my mind. It's hard to imagine your father when you don't know the tiniest thing about him*. Jeanette didn't even have any photos of him.

'Well,' said Jeanette, 'he was short. Not shorter than

me, but short for a man. Probably explains why you're such a petite little thing. He used to wear his hair a bit too long. I was always telling him to get it cut, but it was the fashion at the time.' Her gaze swept up to the TV even though it wasn't on. 'He was so funny. Used to have me in fits of giggles all the time. And then he'd suddenly be all serious and give me this look – well, never mind.'

Fliss watched her mother with a growing feeling of sympathy. When she talked about Fliss's father, Jeanette's face took on a younger look – a softer look. It was almost as though by remembering her youth, she became younger again. What was she like when she was a teenager? Was she happier? More carefree?

'We were at school when we started going out,' Jeanette went on. 'Silly little things we were, always holding hands in class and sneaking kisses behind the bike shed. And then we both left school at sixteen and tried to get jobs. But it was hard. There wasn't much around at the time. He had better exam results than I did, but I was the one who got the sales job. They said they gave me the job because I was persuasive and convincing.' She laughed suddenly. 'It was funny really because inside I was terrified, but somehow I always knew what to say.'

'A bit like acting,' said Fliss.

Jeanette looked at her as though she'd forgotten Fliss was in the room. 'Yes, I suppose. Never thought of it that way. Anyway, he didn't get a job for ages. I used to pay for things for him when we went out. He didn't like that. And I guess maybe I should have seen the signs then. But I was still – well, I still believed we were going to be together. Then a couple of friends asked if we wanted to share a house with them. They had a spare room. So we moved in together. I was only seventeen. My parents were scandalized.' She smiled briefly. 'Mum said she'd never speak to me again if we didn't get married. I told her that was so old-fashioned and who needed a bit of paper to prove they were in love? But she kept on at me, and in the end I suppose I mentioned it so many times that he got annoyed with me. He said we were too young, we didn't earn enough money, we shouldn't rush into that kind of thing. So I tried not to mention it, for ages.' She paused. 'And then I found out I was pregnant.'

There was a pause. Fliss twisted her fingers together. Her mother hadn't mentioned her father's name once. Fliss knew what it was – Robert – but it seemed Jeanette found it easier to talk about him if she didn't have to say his name. So much of this story was new to her, Fliss didn't want to break the spell. 'What happened next?' she prompted quietly.

'Well,' said Jeanette, 'that was that, wasn't it? Off he went. Thought I was trying to trap him into marriage – that's what he said. Turned out he'd been having a bit on the side too. I was the only one who didn't know. Wish I'd found out earlier. I wouldn't have wasted my time.'

'Did you – how did you feel about me?' Fliss asked hesitantly. 'When you knew you were going to be on your own, I mean.'

'Mum said I told you so, of course,' said Jeanette. 'She let me move back in for a while, until you were born. But she kept saying I needed to stand on my own two feet. She looked after you while I went out to work – to start with, anyway. It was very hard. I worked all day and then when I came home, I had to look after you.' She looked at Fliss and there was a weariness in her expression. 'You were a bad sleeper,' she said. 'You didn't sleep right through the night until you were nearly two. And then you had nightmares. You used to creep into my bed in the middle of the night and cry.' She blinked. 'But I kept us going.' The shine to her eyes disappeared, to be replaced by something harder.

'I kept us off benefits. You never went without. A neighbour said she was going to start being a child minder and she let me have a reduced rate for you. But it was tough. Especially with having no real qualifications. GCSEs aren't enough – not to get up the ladder, not these days. A levels and degrees, that's what you need. That guarantees you a decent salary, at the least.'

Fliss kept quiet. Jeanette hadn't really answered her question, and she wondered why. Had she been unhappy when she discovered she was going to have a baby? Had she considered getting rid of it? Or had she felt a secret delight, knowing there was a new life growing inside her?

'That's why I want the best for you,' Jeanette was continuing, staring hard at Fliss. 'I want you to have the opportunities I didn't. If you want to go to university, then I'll work every hour I have to send you. I just don't want you to end up with no prospects, like me.'

'You have prospects,' said Fliss. 'You have a job.'

'But not one I would have wanted,' Jeanette replied. 'Not one I enjoy. I do what I do because I don't have many options.' She wrinkled her nose. 'I'd give anything for a job like Vivienne's. Or like your friend Victoria's parents. She lives in a lovely big house; her parents must be rolling in it.'

'But they're never there when she comes home from school,' said Fliss gently. 'She has to make do with the au pair. You're always here for me when I get home. Asking me about my day. Making sure I'm all right.'

'That's what mothers are for,' said Jeanette practically.

'Giving me a hug,' said Fliss.

Jeanette stared at her daughter for a moment, and Fliss was astonished to see her eyes shone with tears again. 'I do try,' she said softly. 'I do try to be a good mother. But it's not easy when you're on your own . . .'

'You do a brilliant job,' said Fliss firmly. 'Brilliant.' *Apart from not listening to my dreams*, she thought traitorously to herself.

Jeanette reached out. 'Let's have one of those hugs now.' Fliss went into her arms, and Jeanette sighed again. 'I just want you to fulfil your potential,' she whispered into Fliss's ear. 'You're a bright girl; you do well at school. I know money isn't everything, but there's nothing more reassuring than a stable career. When you've got enough money and a bit over, you can do other things as hobbies. Don't you think?'

'Mmm,' said Fliss.

Jeanette pulled back and framed Fliss's face with her hands. 'Don't live hand-to-mouth like I've done, Felicity. Make something of yourself. Promise me.'

What about acting? said a tiny voice inside Fliss. She nodded and said, 'I promise, Mum.' And after all, maybe her mother was right. There was no money in acting, everyone said. Was it worth the risk for your dream?

♥

'This is the big one,' said Candy. 'The balcony scene. How are you doing with your lines?'

'I know mine,' said Fliss.

Tom looked at her, amused. 'Do you know all the lines in the play?'

Fliss blushed. 'Only Juliet's.'

He laughed. 'You're showing me up, you know. I haven't learned mine yet.'

'It's easy once you get going,' Fliss told him, but something was bothering her. Where was Samantha?

'Samantha had something on tonight,' said Candy, as though reading Fliss's thoughts. 'She can't make it today.' She pretended she didn't see the relief on Fliss's face. 'Well, let's take it from the top and see how we go.' She indicated the floor, where some strips of coloured tape had been laid out. 'Obviously we don't have a real balcony yet, but we will do on the set. I've marked the floor so you can see where it will be. Fliss, you will go round the back of the set to the ladder. The balcony isn't going to be that high off the ground – about eight feet – but it'll be high enough to hurt yourself if you fall off. There won't be much room up there, so just be careful.'

'OK.'

'Now,' said Candy, 'this is the second time Romeo and Juliet have met, but this time they can't physically reach each other. It's incredibly frustrating for them. Also, Juliet keeps being called away, so their conversation is interrupted. I'll do the off-stage lines for the moment. Fliss, here's a chair. If you pretend the back of it is the rail of the balcony . . .'

Gradually, they started to stumble through the scene. Candy interrupted them often, saying, 'Try to move about a bit, Tom. You're a bit stuck in that corner now,' and 'Fliss, just because the audience won't be able to see your feet doesn't mean you can stand pigeon-toed.'

It was a difficult scene, much harder than Fliss had realized. Confined to the small space of the balcony, she couldn't move around much, and after a while she realized she was waving her arms around all the time in compensation. She made a noise of annoyance and stopped halfway through her speech.

'What's the matter, Fliss?' asked Candy.

'I hate it up here,' said Fliss. 'I can't do anything!'

Candy looked thoughtful. 'I think that's where the intensity comes from. Because you have this barrier, this obstacle between you.'

'But I can't even walk about!' exclaimed Fliss. 'And Tom can't talk to me without turning his back on the audience!'

'That's true,' said Tom. 'I can't face you properly because you're behind me all the time.'

They looked at Candy. She grinned. 'Fine. Then play the scene without the balcony.'

'What?' Fliss was puzzled.

'Pretend there's no balcony.' Candy spread her hands. 'Just for now. In fact, pretend there's no audience either. Just do the scene as if you'd met in the garden.'

Fliss looked at Tom. 'What do you think?'

He smiled. 'I'm game if you are.'

'Do it with the script if you have to,' said Candy,

'but try not to read too much. Use it as a prop, not to rely on.'

'OK.' Fliss took up a seated position on the floor, and Tom glanced at his script. 'But soft! What light through yonder window breaks? It is the east, and Juliet is the sun!'

Fliss began to giggle. Tom stopped. 'What?'

'You can't stand there,' said Fliss. 'I can see you. Surely the point is that I don't know you're there for ages.'

'Oh, sorry. Good point.' Tom looked around. 'I need something to hide behind.' Candy watched in amusement as Tom grabbed a couple of chairs and balanced one on the other. Then he ducked down behind them. 'Better?'

'Much better,' said Fliss.

It was the silliest balcony scene ever performed. Tom darted from chair to chair in order to stay out of sight, finally crashing through a pile of them to reveal himself. Fliss had trouble saying her lines, she was laughing so much. Both of them became more and more over the top, declaiming their lines as if in a pantomime.

By the time they reached 'O blessed, blessed night,' Candy had had enough. 'Stop!'

Fliss and Tom, flushed and weak with laughter,

turned to look at her. 'Oh,' said Fliss, 'but I haven't even got to "Hist!" yet. I was looking forward to that bit.'

'I think that's enough, don't you?' said Candy, trying to sound stern, although a little smile hovered around her mouth. 'It was very funny, guys, but this is meant to be a deeply romantic scene. I thought taking away set and audience restrictions might loosen it up a bit, but I wasn't expecting *Carry On Romeo*.' She chewed her lip for a moment. 'I think you'd better take a few minutes to calm down. Go get some fresh air or something. Come back in five minutes and we'll do it again – back on set.'

Fliss and Tom obediently went out of the room, casting guilty glances at Candy. 'It's raining,' said Fliss, when they reached the front doors of the building.

'We can stand under the porch thing,' said Tom. So they went out onto the concrete area and looked up at the perspex roof, which was running with water.

'Hope it doesn't rain when we're performing,' said Fliss. 'What would we do?'

'Keep going, I guess,' said Tom. 'Unless it got really heavy. Then I suppose we'd have to stop.'

'We could do it indoors somewhere,' said Fliss.

Tom shook his head. 'Where? We're going to be in the park, remember?'

'There's that bandstand thing . . .'

'You'd never fit us and the audience under there. It's too small.'

'Hmm. Candy must have somewhere in mind. She said so.' Fliss looked up at the roof. 'I love rain.'

Tom looked at her curiously. 'Why?'

Fliss shrugged. 'I don't know. I love being indoors, sitting by the window, watching the rain run down the glass. It's – cosy, somehow.'

'Ah,' said Tom. 'You like rain if you're not out in it. That's different.'

'Well yeah,' said Fliss. 'I like watching it – not getting wet. And I hate thunderstorms.'

Tom's face lit up. 'I love them! All that thunder crashing around. Bam! Blam! Bazam!'

Fliss laughed. 'You say it like you're playing the drums.'

'I do play the drums,' said Tom.

'Do you?'

'Yeah. Not very well though. I don't think I'm coordinated enough. You've got to get each arm and leg doing something different all at the same time.' Tom mimed playing an imaginary drumkit, and tangled his arms together. 'Mad. If you start think-ing about what you're doing it all goes wrong.'

'I don't play any instruments,' said Fliss. 'I wanted

to play the flute but my mum wouldn't let me. Said it would disturb the neighbours.'

'I could see you playing the flute,' said Tom, looking at her critically. 'Like a little elf or something.'

'A what?'

'An elf. No, hear me out – you've got a sort of pixie face, and your ears are a bit pointed . . . what?'

Fliss had gone red. It was one thing to be talking about music; it was quite another to have Tom examining her face as though she were some kind of experiment. She mumbled something at her feet.

Tom laughed. 'Oh, don't take offence. I mean it nicely. You're a very sweet pixie – and you should be playing a little flute. Like Pan. You know, that garden spirit thing with hooves and panpipes. I could see you as that. And dancing.'

Fliss couldn't help giggling. 'Dancing? Me? Now you *are* being silly.'

'And you've got a pixie giggle too,' said Tom, smiling at her. 'Maybe you grant wishes or something.'

'Wishes?'

'Yeah, you know – to help people out. Heal the sick. Make people fall in love.' He suddenly stopped, and looked away. There was an awkward silence. Fliss's fingers tingled. An odd atmosphere had descended and she found it impossible to look at Tom. That was a strange thing for him to say, wasn't it? What did he mean? Make people fall in love? Who . . .

The door banged behind them, making them both jump. 'Hey, daydreamers!' said Candy. 'Ready to go again?'

Silently, Tom gestured for Fliss to go first, and the three of them headed back to the studio.

'You two OK?' asked Candy, staring at them.

Fliss shook herself. 'Fine. We were talking about drums.'

'And rain,' added Tom. Fliss sneaked a glance at him and was relieved to see him looking more like his usual self.

'Right,' said Candy, 'let's take it from the top. And no silliness this time.'

Fliss had never felt less like being silly. All of the inside of her head felt like it was taken up with Tom's words just before they came in. He had called her a pixie – was that a good thing? He'd said it with a kind of affection . . .

'Fliss! Your line!'

'Sorry.' Fliss dragged her mind out of the previous conversation and tried to concentrate.

'That was about a million times better,' said Candy at the end. 'We still need to sort out some blocking issues, but basically it's taking shape.' She looked at her watch. 'I'm sorry, guys, I need to run. Good work today – maybe it helped to be totally silly and over the top. Got it out of the way. It's very natural to laugh when you're embarrassed or a bit uneasy.' She smiled. 'But it's looking really promising now. I must dash – learn those lines!' She grabbed her bag and went.

Tom looked at Fliss. 'I thought that went really well today. Nice to be a bit silly. All this tragedy stuff – it's so . . . well . . .'

'Tragic?' said Fliss.

'Exactly,' said Tom.

They walked together to the front doors. 'Rain's stopped,' said Tom. 'So that's all right.'

'Yeah,' said Fliss.

They stood awkwardly for a moment. 'Well,' said Fliss.

'You – uh – you want to get a bite to eat?' said Tom. 'I missed dinner at home, and it's still light. We could go get a burger or something.'

Panic flooded Fliss like a tidal wave. 'Oh,' she said in a strangled voice, 'I think my mum's expecting me home.'

'Half an hour?' suggested Tom. 'You could ring her.'

Fliss's throat closed in terror. Go for a burger with

Tom? Like a *date*? She'd never be able to eat anything! 'Sorry,' she said, and shifted her bag on her shoulder. 'Got to get back. See you soon!' And without even meeting his gaze, she walked as fast as she could until she was out of sight.

Chapter 7

what's the worst that can happen?

'You did WHAT?' shrieked Mari. 'I cannot *believe* you, Fliss Richards! You turned him *down*?'

Fliss stared miserably at the floor. 'I know. I don't know what happened.' She glanced helplessly at Victoria. 'You know what I'm like.'

But Victoria too was looking baffled. 'But you like him. You *really* like him, I mean. I know you pretend not to, but you like him more than we do, I think.' She saw Fliss's face and reached out to give her a hug. 'You big silly. You can't hide things like that from your best friends. But if you like him that much, why on earth did you say no?'

Fliss shook her head. 'I just froze. I didn't know what to say. I mean, what would we talk about?'

'Oh, I don't know,' said Mari sarcastically. 'Drumming, maybe, or the play, or HOW MUCH YOU LIKE HIM – *anything*!' She shook her head. 'Well, that's it. You've blown it.'

'Oh God,' said Fliss. 'I have, haven't I?' She sat down heavily on Victoria's bed. The three of them had retreated to Victoria's room after the rain had spoiled their afternoon sunbathe in the garden. 'I don't know what's wrong with me. I think about him all the time. It's ridiculous! I even dream about him! And then − in real life he asks me out. And I say no!' She buried her head in her hands. 'I am such an idiot.'

Victoria sat down next to her. 'You're not an idiot. You're just shy. I can see why you might have been scared. But he doesn't know that.'

'He probably thinks you're not interested,' said Mari, biting into an apple.

Fliss looked up, her eyes wide. 'But I am. I couldn't be more interested.'

Mari shrugged. 'Then your only chance is to talk to him about it. Say you made a mistake. Ask him out.'

Fliss went white. 'Do what? I can't do that!'

Victoria sighed. 'See, there you go again. Fliss, I know you're a bit scared of this kind of thing . . .'

'A bit?' interrupted Mari. Victoria shot her a look and she subsided. 'All right, all right.'

'But maybe it's time to start taking a few more risks,' Victoria went on.

'But how?' Fliss was distressed. 'What if things go wrong?'

'What's the worst that can happen?' asked Victoria.

'Oh, I don't know,' said Fliss. 'Tom could tell me he thinks I'm the ugliest person on the planet, he'd never go out with me in a million years, then he turns away and everyone starts laughing and I'll be completely humiliated and everyone on the bus will say for months: Look there's that girl who made such a fool of herself over Tom Mayerling.'

There was a short silence. 'Well,' said Victoria, 'if you put it like that . . .'

'I've got an idea,' said Mari. 'It's like acting, isn't it? I mean, when you act on stage, Fliss, you become someone else. You've told us – it's like the real world goes away, right?'

Fliss nodded. 'Yes.'

'So why can't you do that in real life?' Mari was triumphant. 'You just have to pretend to be someone else – someone more confident.'

'Of course!' Victoria was excited. 'It's easy that way! You just act a character when you're asking Tom out.'

'But I'm not someone else then,' objected Fliss. 'I'm

me. And if I wasn't me, then I wouldn't be asking him out, would I?' Her two friends looked puzzled. Fliss tried to explain. 'It doesn't work like that. I can do it on stage. I've got lines, I know what I have to say. I'm being someone who's not me. They do things I wouldn't do, they say things I wouldn't say. But it's not real. It's theatre. This is real – this is my life.' Her eyes filled with tears. 'I can't change the way I am. It's just not me.'

'Oh, sweetie.' Victoria put her arms around Fliss and gave her a squeeze. 'We know, and we love you just the way you are. And we did promise we wouldn't bully you into changing anything.' She glared at Mari, who looked guilty. 'Listen, if Tom really likes you then he'll ask you out again. I'm sure.'

Mari looked less certain. 'He might. But maybe he's not the right boy for you anyway. I mean, if he asked you out and you said no, maybe deep down your subconscious was trying to tell you something.'

Fliss wiped her eyes. 'You really think so?'

'Yes, I do,' said Mari firmly.

'Well, I still think he likes you,' said Victoria. 'All that stuff he said about you being a pixie – that's a compliment.'

'Is it?'

'Yes. Pixies are cute. And if he does like you, then he won't give up.' She squeezed Fliss again. 'And next time you can say yes, right?'

♥

Fliss spent the next few days trying to imagine how she would respond to Tom if he asked her out again. Jeanette was rather astonished to catch her daughter one day sitting in front of the mirror and saying firmly, 'Yes, I would love to, thank you.'

'Everything OK?' asked Jeanette.

Fliss went red. 'Yes, fine,' she said, scrambling up.

'You rehearsing or something?'

'Uh – yes, that's right.'

Jeanette looked quizzical. 'Didn't sound very Shakespearean.'

'It's – um – an acting exercise.' Fliss waved her hand. 'You wouldn't be interested.'

Jeanette smiled. 'Fair enough. I just wanted to let you know I've invited Vivienne to dinner on Friday.'

'Oh,' said Fliss. Dinner with Vivienne. Just what she wanted. 'All right.'

Jeanette put her head on one side. 'You done something different with your hair?'

Fliss lifted her hand to her head automatically. 'No, why?'

'No reason. You look – different somehow. Taller. Are you wearing heels?'

'No.'

'Oh well.' Jeanette raised her eyebrows. 'Just me going mad, obviously. I'll be downstairs if you need me.'

Fliss closed the door behind her mother and took a closer look in the mirror. Was she taller? Or was it all this practising she was doing? Could she maybe, just maybe, be feeling a little more confident? She tried smiling at herself. Was that a confident smile? *Put your shoulders back*, she told herself. *Chin up. Face the world confidently. There you go. That's more like it. That's the kind of person who would say yes to Tom Mayerling. Isn't it?*

In the midst of her self-examination, her mobile rang. 'Mari,' said Fliss. 'You OK?'

'Yeah.' Mari's voice sounded strange. 'I had a rehearsal today.'

'Oh yes – the Nurse meets Romeo scene?'

'Yeah, that's right.' Mari fell silent.

'Did it go OK?' prompted Fliss, wondering what all this was about.

'Yes, it was fine,' said Mari. 'But, Fliss – I've got something to tell you.'

'What?'

'Well – it looks like Tom is going out with Samantha.'

Fliss's stomach seemed to drop through the floor. 'What?' she whispered.

'I know. I didn't believe it at first, but she was all over him at the rehearsal. And then – well, are you sure you want to hear this?'

'Yes.' Fliss sank onto her bed. This was it – this was her punishment for turning him down the other day. 'Tell me everything.'

'Well, Samantha came in looking like the cat that got the cream. All soft and purring. I nearly punched her silly face in, she was so annoying. Kept saying "Oh, Tom, did I leave my script at yours yesterday?" And picking imaginary bits of dirt off his T-shirt. She kept interrupting as we were doing the scene too, giving Tom advice and calling him "honey" all the time. Even Candy got annoyed. Told her if she couldn't keep quiet, she'd have to go outside.'

Fliss swallowed. 'Did it work?'

'Yeah, for a while. We got the scene done anyway. I have to say, Fliss, I can see why you like him so much. I know I've always said he's good-looking, but there's more to him than that. He really listens properly when you say something. Most boys pretend they're listening, but they're not really – they're waiting for you to stop talking so they can say whatever it is they want to say.'

'Mari . . .'

'Yes, sorry. Anyway, my point is that I made a suggestion in the scene, and Tom was really nice about it. It didn't work, what I said, but he was willing to have a go. Not all stuck up about it. Samantha didn't like it – in fact, I think it was because of her that my idea didn't work, but never mind.' Mari took a breath. 'We got to the end of the rehearsal, and I was pretty shattered. The Nurse does a lot of waffling in that scene, and Candy's directed it so that Tom and the other boys do a lot of skipping around me, if you see what I mean. I get pulled from one side of the stage to the other. So by the time Candy called it a day, I was gasping for some water. I went out into the corridor – you know that water fountain thing they've got? The one you should never let your lips touch in case you catch something? I swear

103

they should get a proper water cooler thingy . . .'

'Mari!'

'Sorry. So I was having a drink there, and all the others came out of the studio except Tom and Samantha. And I'd left my bag in there, so I had to go back. And . . . oh, Fliss, I'm so sorry.'

Fliss closed her eyes. 'Just tell me.'

'They were there. The two of them – standing in the middle of the room. Snogging each other's face off.'

Fliss hadn't even realized she'd been holding her breath, but now she let it out in a shallow sigh.

'Fliss? You still there?' Mari waited for a moment, but Fliss didn't reply. 'I'm so sorry, Fliss. They're definitely together. Samantha looked up and saw me watching, and she just smiled at me. I mean – ooh, I was so mad. On your behalf, I mean. She's such a cat. She's had her claws into Tom for weeks. And I guess – well – I guess he's finally given in to her.' Mari paused again, but Fliss was still silent. 'He doesn't deserve you,' said Mari. 'He's not worth it. If he can be taken in by a – a weasel like Samantha, then—'

'Thanks for letting me know,' said Fliss in a small voice.

'Oh, Fliss, don't be sad. He's not worth it, really.

There'll be someone better just round the corner. I know it.'

'Yeah.' Fliss hung up.

♥

'You OK?' asked Tom. 'You look a bit – I dunno. Ill or something.'

'I'm fine,' said Fliss. For the first time since rehearsals started, she wished she wasn't playing Juliet. Any part but that. She'd even gladly swap with Victoria and be in the Chorus. Anything so that she didn't have to look at Tom as though she were in love with him. Knowing all the time she couldn't have him. It felt like months since she'd heard the news about Tom and Samantha, but in reality it was only ten days. Ten days in which she'd cried herself to sleep, attended a rehearsal with Mari, concentrated so hard on her lines she'd left her bag behind in the studio . . . Fliss felt as though she was the unluckiest person in the world. The joy of getting the part of Juliet now felt like a dream. This rehearsal was going to be a nightmare.

To make matters worse, Samantha was in her usual corner and staring intensely at Fliss again. Even when Fliss had her back to Samantha, she could feel the stare burning through her shoulder blades. It was giving her a headache.

Candy also peered at Fliss. 'You do look a bit peaky. Are you feeling under the weather?'

Fliss shook her head. 'I'm fine. Honestly.'

'I'll reschedule the rehearsal if necessary,' said Candy. 'Though actually we're on a tight one as it is. I'm not sure there's much extra time available.'

'I said I'm fine,' snapped Fliss. 'Can we just get on with it?' She was being unreasonable, she knew. But there was simply no point postponing the rehearsal; it would have to be done at some point. And Fliss had too much professional pride to make things difficult for Candy. She bit her lip, tried to ignore the smirk on Samantha's lips, and turned to focus on Candy.

'Right,' said Candy, 'well, if you're OK then, we'll make a start. Now, it's the morning after the night before, if you see what I mean. Romeo and Juliet have got married. He's killed her cousin, but she's so deeply in love with him she can't give him up. He's about to be banished from the area, so she doesn't know when she'll see him again. They've consummated their marriage – you know what that means?'

Fliss and Tom nodded. Fliss blushed.

'So,' said Candy. 'They've slept together for the first time – it's a big deal for Juliet in particular. And they've woken up quite early, and Romeo needs to be off very quickly, because if he's found in the area he could be executed.'

The door banged and Mari came in. 'Sorry I'm late,' she said, flustered. 'Got on the wrong bus by mistake.'

Samantha snorted. Mari ignored her.

'Take a seat,' said Candy. 'You're not on for a while anyway.' She turned back to Tom and Fliss. 'I've split this scene for rehearsal purposes because Juliet has a long conversation with her mother after this bit and it seemed daft to have you sitting around for it, Tom. And Sarah's gone down with hayfever, so she's not feeling too great either.' Candy sighed. 'I always think rehearsing in the holidays means that everyone will be able to come to all the rehearsals. But it never works out that way, does it?'

'Is Sarah OK?' asked Fliss. Sarah was playing Lady Capulet, Juliet's mother, and although Fliss and Sarah got on well, Fliss found it very annoying that Sarah kept mixing up her lines. 'Oh, it doesn't matter,' Sarah had said when Fliss had mentioned it. 'As long as you get the general idea across, isn't that the point?' Fliss had bitten her lip and kept quiet.

'I hope so,' said Candy. 'She's got a bright red nose and keeps sneezing, but she said the doctor has given her some new medicine, so let's hope that works.' She gave a rueful smile. 'But one step at a time, right? So let's get on with it. You're both in Juliet's room, and for the purposes of this scene, you have to imagine the window at the back. Romeo goes out of the window halfway through so that he won't be discovered. Right?'

'Right,' said Tom.

It was the hardest thing Fliss had ever had to do. She tried to imagine away the real world, just as she usually did when playing a part. But although she could imagine away Candy and Mari, she still felt the burning of Samantha's gaze.

Candy stopped the rehearsal. 'Fliss, what's wrong? I'm not getting the usual level of performance from you.'

Unconsciously, Fliss's gaze flicked towards Samantha, who was doodling on her script and looking smug. Candy followed her eyes. 'Ah. But we've talked about this, haven't we?'

Fliss nodded miserably. 'I'm sorry. I'll try again.'

They started the scene again, but every time Tom went to touch Fliss – on the arm, on the cheek – she flinched away. After a few moments, her jitters got to him and he stopped trying to touch her at all. 'Tom,' said Candy in exasperation, 'now *you're* doing it.

You're supposed to be in love, you two. You look like you hate each other.'

Tom pulled a face. 'I'm sorry. I guess . . .' His eyes went to Samantha.

She looked up. 'What?'

'Maybe . . .' said Tom hesitantly. 'I mean – you and I are going out.'

'So?' Samantha's gaze hardened.

'Well, it's a bit awkward,' said Tom. 'Doing this scene in front of you.'

Samantha stood up. 'Are you saying you want me to leave?' Her voice was as steely as her eyes.

Fliss felt herself shrink. She hated this kind of confrontation.

'I'm just saying,' Tom went on in a placatory tone, 'that maybe it would be easier if . . .'

'Stop right there,' said Samantha, holding up her hand. 'I get it. You don't want me watching while you snog *her*. Fine. If you can't handle it – if you can't be *professional* . . . well.' Words seemed to fail her. She glared one last time at Fliss, picked up her bag and stomped out, tossing her hair.

There was a short silence. Candy cleared her throat. 'I'm not sure that was entirely the right thing to do, Tom.'

Tom cast an agonized glance at Fliss. 'Sorry,' he said,

although he didn't seem sure what for. 'I mean . . .' He looked at the door. 'I think I should . . .' he said. And then, shaking his head, he went after Samantha.

Mari let out an annoyed sigh. '*What* a drama queen,' she said. 'Honestly.'

'Mari,' said Candy, 'please would you take a short break? I need to have a word with Fliss.'

Mari opened her mouth.

'Now,' said Candy.

Mari shrugged and went out.

'Fliss,' said Candy gently, 'this isn't just about Samantha, is it?' She sighed. 'I think you should tell me how you feel about Tom.'

Fliss went pale. 'What?'

'You like him, don't you? I can see it in the way you look at him – or don't look at him.'

Fliss tried to laugh. 'That's acting.'

'No it isn't. I can tell the difference.' Candy sighed. 'It's impacting on your performance. I see that Samantha and Tom are dating now, right?' She shook her head. 'I don't think it's a great idea while the play is going on, but she can be very persuasive.'

Fliss thought of Mari's description of the two of them kissing in the studio. 'Doesn't seem like he needed much persuading.'

'Maybe he thought she was the only option.' Candy

put her head on one side. 'It's none of my business, Fliss, except that it sort of is because of the play. I can see this has made things more difficult for you. But if you can't play convincingly opposite Tom, well – the whole thing falls apart. I don't have time to re-cast. You know that.'

'I know.'

'So you have to make some kind of decision,' said Candy. 'I know it's hard for you, but if you want to do yourself justice, you have to forget everything that's happening outside the play. Forget Samantha. Forget the fact she's going out with Tom. I know that's hard . . .' Fliss gave a small smile. 'But you have to stay focused.'

Fliss looked down at the floor. *Why is everything so unfair?* she thought. And at the same time, she felt guilty for feeling that way. She was the luckiest girl in the world to have the chance to play Juliet! And it was her own fault she wasn't going out with Tom – she had turned him down, after all. 'Things were a bit easier before . . .'

Candy nodded. 'I know. And you need to remember that in the grown-up theatrical world, these things happen all the time. People are thrown together. They have to pretend to feel very intense emotions. Sometimes that spills over into real life too – people get together, split up, all sorts – but they still have to perform on stage as though none of that is happening.'

'But I'm not in the grown-up theatrical world.'

'Not yet,' said Candy, 'but one day you should be. You have real talent, Fliss. Real natural talent. You have an instinctive ear for dialogue, and you move around the stage so well. But you won't get anywhere without focus. And that kind of goes for real life too.' She took a step back and considered Fliss. 'Maybe this is a time of challenge for you – on and off stage. Focus will give you determination, and determination will give you confidence. Use it.' She smiled suddenly. 'Besides, things change very quickly. Today, Tom and Samantha are going out together. Tomorrow they might not be. But whatever your feelings for him, and whoever he's going out with, you still have to play Juliet to his Romeo. Yes?'

Candy looked quite strict as she said this, but Fliss felt as though she understood in some way. And instead of being saddened, she felt stronger. Candy thought she could do this part. Candy expected certain things from her. She owed it to Candy to behave in a professional manner. Fliss took a breath and lifted her head. 'Yes.'

'Right.' Candy heaved a sigh. 'I suppose I'd better

go out and see what's going on. But I warn you, Fliss, I intend to bring everyone back in here and carry on with the rehearsal. I can't afford to lose time like this.'

Fliss looked at her steadily. 'I'll be ready.'

'Good girl.'

Chapter 8

there's no money in acting

'Oh, didn't I tell you Vivienne was coming round for dinner?' said Jeanette, as the door bell rang and Fliss looked surprised. 'She was so sorry she had to cancel the other week, so we rearranged for tonight.'

'Oh,' said Fliss. That explained why her mother was wearing an apron and trying to concoct some very complicated recipe involving chicken and avocado.

'Can you get the door for me, Felicity?' asked Jeanette, distractedly running her hands through her hair. 'I don't think those avocados were ripe enough . . . I hope they cook properly.'

Fliss went to get the door, marvelling as always how a visit from Vivienne could send her mother into complete hysteria. 'Felicity, sweetheart!' cried Vivienne, kissing her on both cheeks. A waft of expensive perfume flew up Fliss's nose and nearly made her sneeze. 'What is Jeanette cooking? It smells divine!'

Fliss trailed Vivienne into the kitchen. 'Oh goodness!' cried Jeanette, smoothing her hair back with a floury hand. 'You aren't supposed to come in here!'

'Why ever not?' said Vivienne, looking around. 'The kitchen is the heart of the home, I often say. We have many conversations round our kitchen table – life, love, the way of the world. I'm sure it's the same here.'

Fliss looked at her mother, who was nodding. 'Of course, er – of course. All sorts.' Fliss hid a smile. Conversations round their kitchen table consisted mostly of who was going to win *The X Factor*, but Fliss knew her mother would never admit that to Vivienne.

'I brought wine,' said Vivienne. 'It's a French Sauvignon Blanc. I never know whether to trust the ones from Chile. And South Africa is in a dreadful mess. You know where you are with France.'

'I'm sure it'll be lovely,' said Jeanette, rustling around in the drawer for a corkscrew.

Vivienne waved it away. 'Oh, I don't need that. This is a screw cap. All the best wines have screw caps now.'

'Right.' Jeanette was flustered. 'Well. Get the wine glasses out, Felicity.'

As Fliss dug around in the cupboard to find two wine glasses that matched, she heard Vivienne whisper to Jeanette, 'She's looking a bit peaky. What's happened?'

'She won't tell me,' Jeanette whispered back.

'Could be glandular fever,' said Vivienne. 'Cod liver oil, that's what she needs. And ginseng. That'll pep her up. I'll send you some.' She beamed at Fliss as she emerged with the wine glasses. 'Thanks so much.'

'Dinner should be about ten minutes,' said Jeanette, frowning at the oven. 'Or possibly twenty.'

'Are those avocados?' asked Vivienne, spotting the empty skins by the sink. 'Darling, I hope they were really ripe. They're such a pain to cook well.'

Jeanette looked terrified. 'Yes,' she managed.

Fliss came to the rescue. 'Vivienne, would you like to come and sit down in the front room? I'm sure Mum will be through in a moment, won't you?'

'Yes,' said Jeanette, throwing Fliss a grateful look. 'Two secs. I just have to turn out the pudding.'

Vivienne sank into the most comfortable chair in the room and looked critically at Fliss. 'Now don't take this the wrong way,' she said, 'but have you ever thought of doing something else with your hair?'

'My hair?' said Fliss.

'Yes.' Vivienne gestured around her own head. 'It's just that every time I see you, it looks exactly the same. So – straight. Have you ever thought of curling it? Or twisting it up? Even a French plait would add a bit of variety.'

'I don't know how to do a French plait,' said Fliss, reddening.

Vivienne looked at her pityingly. 'Sweetheart, it's easy. You just need a bit of practice and someone to show you how.' She shook her head and smiled. 'My Sofie mastered it in about ten minutes when I showed her. Would you like me to show you too?'

'Oh,' said Fliss, alarmed, 'that's very kind of you, but, um . . .'

Jeanette bustled in from the kitchen, minus her apron. 'Whew!' she said, lifting her glass. 'Good to see you, Vivienne!'

Vivienne raised her own glass in answer. 'You too, Jeanette. Felicity, are you not having any?'

'Felicity doesn't drink,' said Jeanette before Fliss could speak.

'Doesn't drink?' echoed Vivienne in some astonishment. 'But all the young people are out getting drunk these days. Isn't it the fashion?'

Jeanette shook her head. 'Not Fliss. She's never liked it. I gave her some wine on her tenth birthday and she was sick. Wouldn't touch it after that.'

'Well,' said Vivienne. 'I've heard it all now.' She sniffed. 'Can you smell something burning?'

Jeanette jumped up as if she'd been shot. 'The chicken!' she yelped and vanished into the kitchen. 'It's all right!' they heard her call a moment later. 'Caught it just in time! Do sit up at the table and I'll bring it through.'

'Can't wait,' said Vivienne sweetly, and Fliss could have kicked her. *You did that on purpose*, she thought. *Sending Mum off to the kitchen a bundle of nerves. Why do you always do that to people?*

The chicken and avocado turned out surprisingly well, and even Vivienne found it hard to criticize. 'However, dear,' she said, 'I do recommend using a hand blender for making mash – it's the only really certain way of getting out the lumps and you end up with such a creamy consistency.'

Jeanette nodded and smiled through gritted teeth.

'So,' said Vivienne, having offered her opinions

on how Jeanette should update her décor, her own new car and its desirable qualities, the sad death of the old lady next door, ('but at least now the place won't smell so badly of *cats*') and the local hospital ('waiting times are a *disgrace*'), 'Felicity. Jeanette tells me you're doing a little play in the park soon.'

'Yes,' said Fliss. '*Romeo and Juliet.*'

'Oh, Shakespeare,' said Vivienne dismissively. 'Not my favourite playwright. Give me a good Ayckbourn any day. At least you know where you are with him. And *Romeo and Juliet* – how very GCSE. Which part are you playing?'

'Juliet.'

Vivienne's perfectly arched eyebrows climbed into her fringe. 'Really! Aren't you a little young?'

'Juliet is only thirteen,' said Fliss defensively, feeling that this fact made her, if anything, on the old side.

'But didn't I read Judi Dench saying somewhere that in order to really capture the innocence of Juliet, one needed to have experienced the rigours of true love in real life?' Vivienne shook her head. 'Which would of course mean that one would need to be at least twenty before one was qualified.'

Fliss puzzled over this. 'Do you mean you can't be in love before the age of twenty?' she asked hesitantly.

Vivienne looked astonished that her opinion was being questioned. 'Ah,' she said, 'you're talking about *crushes*. Not the same thing at all, I think you'll find.' She sighed. 'I myself had several crushes at school. So did your mother, as I recall – only see how that turned out.'

Jeanette turned scarlet and hastily spooned some mash into her mouth to avoid speaking.

Fliss felt embarrassed on her mother's behalf. 'If you're talking about my father, that wasn't a crush,' she found herself saying. 'He loved her too.'

'I don't want to discuss this right now,' said Jeanette loudly.

'I'm not saying it wasn't *intense*,' said Vivienne, laying a sympathetic hand on Jeanette's. 'But love as a teen is always an immature love. Blind love. You haven't the wisdom to step back and evaluate.' She drew back her hand and smiled in a satisfied way. 'That's why I felt I had to get involved when Sofie brought home a *most* unsuitable boy. Of course, that was a long time ago now.'

'How is she getting on?' asked Jeanette quickly, delighted to be able to switch topics.

'Well.' Vivienne sat back and prepared to talk about her second favourite topic – her daughter. 'She's having a tough time at the moment, I gather.

Teacher training is so paper-heavy these days. And they do insist on giving you placements in inner-city schools, where it's more about crowd control than teaching. But from what she tells me, she's doing superbly well. Distinctions or whatever they are in her exams. And all her observations and assessments are outstanding.'

'Teaching sounds very stressful,' remarked Jeanette.

'It is,' said Vivienne, 'but I keep saying if she sticks with it, the rewards will be great. She can have her pick of the jobs. And she teaches English! Well, there'll always be a need for English teachers, won't there? She thought she wanted to do Science, but she soon realized English was a better idea.'

I bet you made her do English, thought Fliss. *Even though she wanted to do Science. And I bet that boy she brought home wasn't unsuitable at all. You just didn't like him, so you told her to get rid of him.* For a sudden moment, she felt absurdly grateful that Vivienne wasn't her mother.

Vivienne's gaze settled on Fliss. 'And what are you going to be when you grow up?'

Fliss's eyes darted towards her mother. 'I haven't decided,' she mumbled.

'Oh, come on now,' said Vivienne indulgently. 'What are you good at?'

'She always gets top grades in French and Spanish,' said Jeanette.

Vivienne's eyes brightened. 'There you are! Languages in the modern world are going to be absolutely *invaluable*. Goodness knows the amount of jobs that are available to people who can speak another language. You could be a translator. Or, or . . .' Vivienne's imagination faltered, 'or a *spook*!'

'A what?'

'A spook!' Vivienne was almost falling off her chair with excitement. 'You know – MI5! The security services! They always want bright young things with language skills. Oh, Jeanette, just think.' Vivienne nodded. 'Your Felicity could be saving the country.'

Jeanette's eyes were round. 'Fancy that,' she breathed. 'I never thought of something like that. Of course, you see them on the television. Go into Parliament sometimes, they do. Advise the Prime Minister.'

Both of them sat back and stared at Fliss, who felt distinctly uncomfortable. A slightly worried look came over Jeanette's face. 'Of course,' she murmured, 'it doesn't seem very – well, very *Felicity*, if you see what I mean.'

'I do see what you mean,' said Vivienne, 'but on the other hand, what a wonderful opportunity. It would open so many doors.'

'She'd be set up for life,' said Jeanette.

'Easily,' agreed Vivienne. 'What do you think, Felicity?'

Fliss jumped at being directly addressed for the first time. 'Me?'

'You could have your own flat in London,' pressed Vivienne. 'You'd be doing something so worthwhile. Using your language skills.'

Fliss hesitated. 'I don't really enjoy languages much.'

'But if you're so good at them, it seems a terrible waste not to use them,' said Vivienne. 'Don't you think?'

'It does sound a bit exciting,' admitted Fliss, though a small part of her was shouting, *No, no! I want to go on the stage!*

'I think it sounds marvellous,' said Jeanette. 'Next time I'm at Parents' Evening, I'll have a word with that careers adviser.'

Fliss felt as though the whole conversation was gathering speed, accelerating down a track she didn't want to take. She gulped. 'I – I do have another idea,' she said. 'About my career, that is.'

Vivienne and Jeanette looked up expectantly. 'Yes?'

Fliss crossed her fingers. 'I'd like to be an actor.'

There was a moment's pause. 'A what?' said Vivienne. Jeanette sighed.

'An actor,' said Fliss.

'Act*ress*,' said Vivienne firmly. 'Female actors are actresses.'

Fliss shook her head. 'Not any more. Everyone's called an actor now. Like firefighters and police officers.'

'Which are at least proper jobs,' said Vivienne. 'Whereas acting is not.' She turned to Jeanette. 'Is she serious?'

'I don't know,' said Jeanette. 'I hope not.'

Vivienne turned back to Fliss and spoke quietly and carefully, as if to a small child or a deaf granny. 'There's no money in acting. There's no security. What makes you think you could make it when thousands don't?'

'I could try,' said Fliss.

Vivienne took a slurp of wine. 'Not good enough. It's all about who's sleeping with whom—'

'Vivienne!'

'She's got to hear the truth, Jeanette. It's not what you know, Felicity, it's who you know. It's all about getting the lucky break.'

Vivienne's assertiveness was like being smothered by a large blanket. *Is this what it's like for Sofie?* 'My director thinks I'm talented,' whispered Fliss.

Vivienne gave her a pitying look. 'Of course she does, sweetheart. She's a college teacher, isn't she? I can't imagine she has much experience of the theatre world herself. She's probably delighted to have someone who remembers their lines and doesn't bump into the furniture.'

'It's called a set,' mumbled Fliss rebelliously. 'And she used to work for the BBC.'

Vivienne's face fell slightly at the prestigious name. 'Well, things are different in TV. And anyway, Felicity, I'm sure you'll change your mind by the time you leave school. When I was your age I wanted to be all sorts of things!' She gave a tinkling laugh and poured herself another glass of wine. 'I even remember wanting to be an acrobat!'

'Why didn't you?' asked Fliss.

'My dear, nobody really does that,' said Vivienne. 'It was just one of those childish fantasies.' She leaned forward and patted Fliss on the shoulder. Fliss winced. 'I think it's lovely that you like drama so much. It'll help bring you out of yourself. But it's not really a career. You can do it as a hobby.'

'That's what I said,' said Jeanette, relieved that her superior friend was backing her up. 'Get a proper job, one with security and stability, and join an amateur company on the side.'

'Exactly,' said Vivienne, nodding. 'A much more sensible way of doing things. Your mother has the right idea, Felicity. You should listen to her.' She smiled at Fliss. 'Mothers always know best.'

Chapter 9

were you holding back for some reason?

Fliss had been surprised to receive a message from Candy, asking her to come to an extra rehearsal. But in many ways she was relieved. Since the evening with Vivienne, Jeanette had referred to Fliss's acting aspirations more than once, and not in a positive way. Fliss was becoming tired of hearing her mother's opinion on 'showbiz' as she called it. Every time there was a magazine photo of a Z-list celebrity falling drunkenly out of a taxi, Jeanette would say with arched eyebrows, 'That's what you get for mixing with showbiz people.' Every time there was a reality TV programme on, Jeanette would comment that 'people only want to be famous these days, talent counts for nothing'. And whenever there was a soap on, Jeanette would say with a horrified fascination that she couldn't see why anyone would want to act in one of 'those things' anyway – 'they're all full of such dreadful people'. She had even declared that she would no longer watch *The X Factor* 'because I feel sorry for them, really. We shouldn't laugh at them.'

Fliss knew this sudden onslaught was only down to Vivienne's recent visit, but it was beginning to get her down. Was it such a bad thing to want to do? After a while, she felt fuzzy in the head with all the conflicting opinions. Her heart told her that she belonged on the stage. But her head wasn't in the clouds. She knew there wasn't much money in acting as a career – not unless you were success-ful on TV or in films, or you worked in the West End on a long-running show. But surely there were ways to scrape by? She didn't mind not having lots of money. That wasn't what life was about, was it? But Jeanette didn't seem to agree. And, watching her mother anxiously pore over the supermarket receipt to see where she'd spent an extra £2.61, Fliss wondered whether maybe she was being the ridiculous one. Her mother had a point. Life was easier if you had money. But still . . .

Thinking so much about her future career had almost pushed thoughts of Tom out of Fliss's head, but when she saw him at the extra rehearsal, her stomach did that strange wibbly thing it always did.

'It's just the three of us,' said Candy. She glanced at the two of them. 'No Samantha today.'

'What scene are we doing?' asked Tom, script in hand.

'We're not,' said Candy. 'We're doing improvisation.'

Fliss's stomach wibbled even more.

Tom looked puzzled. 'What for?'

'I think the two of you need to get back to basics,' said Candy. 'When rehearsals started, there was a real chemistry between you onstage. But recently other things seem to have got in the way.' Fliss glanced sideways at Tom, who caught her eye and then looked away quickly. 'I think we need to recapture that feeling you had to start with,' Candy went on. 'So we're going to do some improvisation without scripts. Just two people meeting and falling in love.'

Oh no, thought Fliss. This was far too close to her real feelings!

'I think we need to keep it in the Shakespearean setting,' said Candy, 'rather than making it too contemporary. So you're still Romeo and Juliet, and you're still meeting at a party, but this time I want you to make it up as you go along. You don't have to stick to the style of the script or even what happens in the original scene. Just go with the flow.'

Fliss felt panicked. 'Just go straight into it?'

Candy smiled at her. 'You want to do some warm-ups first, Fliss?'

'Uh . . .' Fliss looked at Tom. 'Well, I don't know . . .'

Tom caught her eye. 'Maybe we should just go for it,' he said. Then he grinned. 'Besides, it's meant to be awkward. We've never met. And it's a party. I'm always awkward at parties.'

Fliss smiled in relief, though she didn't believe him for a minute. 'Me too.'

'Save it for the scene,' said Candy. 'Right. Off you go.'

Fliss closed her eyes briefly. The room disappeared and re-formed itself. There was a band in the corner, playing something cheerful. Some people were dancing, but she was the daughter of the household and no one had asked her yet. She opened her eyes, and Juliet carefully sat down on a chair, arranging her skirts around her.

'Excuse me,' said a voice.

Juliet looked up to see a tall boy with dark hair and bewitching eyes. She felt her face redden. 'Yes?'

'Is this seat taken?'

'No.'

'Great,' said the boy. 'Then you won't mind if I take it.' He picked it up and turned away.

Juliet's mouth fell open. The boy looked over his shoulder at her and laughed. 'Sorry. Just kidding.' He sat down next to her. 'I like your mask.'

Juliet touched her face; of course, she was wearing a little mask decorated with peacock feathers that just covered the upper part of her face. 'Thank you. I made it myself.'

'Are you as pretty as that underneath?' teased the boy.

Juliet felt embarrassed. 'I don't think so,' she said.

'I'm sure you're even prettier,' said the boy.

'Well, now I can't possibly take off the mask,' said Juliet, 'in case I disappoint you.'

The boy laughed, a genuine sound of merriment. Juliet felt her own mouth curve up in response. 'What's your name?' he asked.

Behind her mask, Juliet felt bold. 'Can't you guess?'

'Hmm.' The boy stared at her in mock solemnity. 'Something ravishing, I expect. Columbine? Rosamund?'

Juliet giggled. 'Nothing so fancy.'

'Nothing fancy,' said the boy. 'Right. Peggy? Susan? Kate?'

Juliet laughed again. This boy was so amusing! And so good-looking too! 'Yes,' she said. 'That last one. That sounds about right.'

'Kate?' said the boy. 'Are you sure?'

Juliet considered for a moment. 'It'll do for now.'

'Methinks you are jesting,' said the boy, but his blue eyes were sparkling. 'Fair enough. Kate it is. See if you can guess *my* name.'

'I couldn't possibly.'

'Oh, go on. I just made a fool of myself over your name. Guess at least one.'

Juliet bit her lip for a moment, and then said, 'Percival.'

'Ha! Wrong.'

'Rupert.'

'No.'

'Paris.'

'I should hope not. That's a ludicrous name.'

'My cousin is called Paris,' said Juliet, trying to sound offended.

'Is he ludicrous?'

'No, actually,' said Juliet. 'He's very nice.'

'I bet he fancies you,' said the boy.

'No he doesn't,' said Juliet. 'He's a friend.'

'Boys and girls can't be friends,' said the boy.

'Of course they can,' said Juliet.

'Keep guessing.'

Juliet sighed. 'Oh, I don't know. Is it something really silly?'

The boy nodded. 'You couldn't get sillier.'

'Oh – I don't know – Humperdink,' said Juliet.

The boy stared for a moment, and then nodded. 'That's it! How did you guess?'

There was a short pause, and then they both fell about laughing. 'You're not serious,' said Juliet through her giggles.

'No,' said the boy, 'but then neither are you, right, Kate?' His laughter suddenly stopped and he reached out a hand to touch her mask. 'Show me. Please. Take it off.'

Juliet felt the heat rise to her face again. 'Oh, I don't think—' she started to say, but the boy put his hand over hers unexpectedly.

'Please,' he said simply.

Juliet reached up to her mask and slid the ribbon over the back of her head. It slipped easily over her silky hair. Then she lifted off the mask.

'But you're beautiful,' said the boy softly. 'Why are you hiding under a mask?'

'It's a masked ball, remember?' she replied.

The boy shook his head. 'You should never wear a mask. You're far too pretty.' He reached out a hand and gently touched her cheek. 'So soft. And if your cousin Paris isn't in love with you then he's as blind as a bat.'

Juliet tried to speak, but no words came. She was mesmerized by his eyes, drawing her in. The music around her faded, and there was only him – the boy. They stared at each other for what felt like hours, and Juliet felt herself begin to lean towards him. But he stayed where he was, and after a moment she stopped. Maybe he didn't want to kiss her after all?

'Lovely,' came Candy's voice, breaking the spell.

Fliss blinked. The room dissolved around her into the bare walls of the studio.

'Some really good work going on there,' said Candy. 'How did it feel?'

Like he loved me, thought Fliss, but even the idea made her blush.

'It felt good,' said Tom. 'Like it was just us and no one else.'

Fliss was startled. 'That's what I felt too.'

He smiled at her. 'Your face completely changed too. It was like you suddenly came alive or something.'

'Really?' She felt embarrassed but pleased.

'How did you feel about the way the scene ended?' asked Candy.

Fliss shifted position on her chair. 'All right.'

Tom flushed. 'It was fine.'

Candy looked from one to the other and then she smiled. 'Really? It felt to me like you should have kissed.'

Tom rubbed his hand through his hair. 'Oh?' he said casually.

Fliss took a deep breath. 'I thought that too.'

'I saw you lean in,' said Candy. 'Tom, were you holding back for some reason? Remember you were being Romeo, not Tom. Romeo is impulsive, he takes the bull by the horns. Or Juliet, in this case.'

Tom rubbed his head again. 'Maybe I'm just not as good as Fliss.'

Fliss turned to him, surprised. 'But you are really good. I really believed you were Romeo.'

'So did I,' agreed Candy.

Tom shrugged. 'I don't know then. It wasn't that I . . .' he faltered slightly. 'It wasn't that I didn't want to . . .' His gaze swept up and caught Fliss's for a moment. She felt a sudden thump in her chest, and her breath stopped in her throat.

There was a slight beeping noise from the corner of the room.

'Sorry, that's my phone,' said Tom.

Candy frowned. 'You know they're meant to be switched off during rehearsals.'

'I know. Sorry. I'll do it now.' Tom went over to his jacket and pulled out his mobile. He read the message, raised his eyebrows slightly and then switched off the phone.

'Problem?' asked Candy, watching him.

'No,' said Tom. 'Just Sam. She wants me to meet her later.'

Sam. Samantha. Fliss felt her breath sink out of her like a deflating balloon. *It wouldn't matter*, she thought, *if he believed I was the best and most beautiful actress in the world. He's still going out with someone else. And it's my own fault for saying no to him in the first place. You don't get a second chance for that kind of thing.*

But then Fliss caught Candy's eye, and she remembered what Candy had said. Off-stage, Tom might be going out with Samantha, but onstage she still had to play Juliet to his Romeo. It might just be acting, but maybe it was better to have that pretend love onstage than not at all.

Even if he was being someone else when he kissed her. Wasn't that better than not being kissed at all?

Chapter 10

it sounds so romantic

'I can't believe it's so hot,' said Mari, trying to rub sun cream into her back. 'Vic, give me a hand, would you? I can't reach the bit between my straps.'

'Do you think it's a good idea to put lotion on just before you go in for your costume fitting?' asked Fliss. 'What if you get your costume all greasy?'

Mari stuck out her tongue. 'It's either that or move into the shade, Little Miss Sensible. Or burn and look like a tomato.'

Fliss grinned. 'Fair enough.' The three girls were stretched out in the hot midday sun on the lawn outside the Arts Centre.

'Typical that we try on costumes on the hottest day of the year,' remarked Mari. 'I'd much rather be lying out here – or preferably in your back garden, Vic – eating ice cream.'

Victoria took the bottle from her and squirted some lotion into her hand. 'We can do that later,' she said. 'When we've finished here.'

Fliss glanced lazily over to the main entrance, where cast members were coming and going. 'Sarah doesn't look very pleased,' she commented, as the girl playing Lady Capulet came out of the doors.

'Hey, Sarah!' called Mari. 'What's yours like?'

Sarah, a tall dark girl with big hands and feet, wandered over, scowling. 'Awful,' she said. 'Mrs Carstairs said they borrowed some costumes from the BBC or something. Candy's got a friend in the wardrobe department there. And Mrs C got all over-excited about it; kept saying we were so lucky to have such *authentic* clothes.' She wrinkled her nose. 'With such *authentic* smells. And it must be strong if I can smell it, because my nose is still stuffed up with hayfever.' She sneezed.

The girls laughed. 'Ew,' said Victoria. 'That sounds disgusting.'

'What's it like to look at though?' asked Fliss. 'Does it look good?'

Sarah shrugged. 'It's OK, I suppose. I was hoping for one of those tall hat things – you know, like in medieval times? But instead I've got something that looks like a blue doughnut to wear on my head.' She looked round at the three girls. 'None of you been in yet?' They shook their heads. 'Well, you're in for a right treat. Just don't say anything to Mrs Carstairs about the smell. She gets all defensive.'

'Thanks for the tip,' said Mari.

'See you tomorrow,' said Sarah. 'Ooh, Fliss – I think I saw your costume while I was in there. It looks really pretty.'

'Really?' said Fliss, pleased.

Sarah nodded. 'Looks like it's got a tiny waist though. Wish I was as petite as you.' She looked ruefully down at herself. 'Being tall is no good if you look like your arms and legs don't fit the rest of you.' She brightened up. 'Still, my costume is so long, you won't be able to see most of me anyway. Bye!'

Victoria finished rubbing cream into Mari's back and snapped the cap onto the bottle. 'Will one of you test me on my lines?'

'You only have six,' said Mari, rolling her eyes. 'Do you still not know them?'

'Eight, actually,' said Victoria, 'and of course I know them, but I'm not sure I *know them* know them, if you know what I mean.'

Fliss laughed at Mari's expression. 'I know what you mean, Victoria. Give me the script. I'll test you.' She found the page and looked up expectantly.

'What?'

'Don't you have the first line?'

'Oh!' Victoria looked startled. 'Oh yes, that's right.' She cleared her throat. 'Two households, both alike in dignity.'

'You've got the very first line of the whole thing?' interrupted Mari. 'Good grief!'

Victoria stopped, annoyed. 'What do you mean, "Good grief"?'

'Well,' said Mari, hastily making her voice sound less sarcastic. 'You said yourself that you're not very confident saying the lines.'

'I never said that,' objected Victoria. 'I said when I act it sounds like I'm saying lines. When Fliss acts it sounds like she just made them up. *That's* what I said.'

'So you're OK about starting the whole entire play then?' asked Mari.

'Stop it,' said Fliss. 'You'll make her nervous.'

'I am fine about it, *actually*,' said Victoria, 'because Candy told me my voice was the strongest and she needed someone with good projection to start the play. And the Chorus isn't really a proper part. It's not a character, it's a narrator. So it doesn't matter if I'm not very good at acting. I just have to be good at speaking. Which I am.' She stuck out her tongue.

Mari grinned. 'You certainly are.'

'Oh, ha ha.'

'Go on then,' said Fliss.

'Go on what?'

'With your lines.'

'Oh! Oh, right. Two households, both alike in dignity, In fair Verona, where we play our scene.'

'Lay,' interrupted Fliss.

Victoria stopped. 'Huh?'

'Where we lay our scene.'

'Is it? No, it can't be. I'm sure it's play our scene.'

Fliss showed her the script. Victoria's face fell. 'Blast. I've been saying it wrong all this time. Why didn't someone tell me?'

'How many of the other eight lines have you learned wrong?' asked Mari, amused.

Victoria flushed. 'None of them.'

'How do you know?' teased Mari. 'Hadn't we better check?'

'I bet you don't know all your lines,' Victoria retorted hotly.

'Do too,' said Mari.

'Go on then.'

'All right.' Mari lay back, stared at the sky, and recited very fast: 'Now by my maidenhead at twelve year old I bade her come. What lamb! What ladybird! – God forbid! – Where's this girl? What, Juliet! Your mother. Faith, I can tell her age unto an hour. I'll lay fourteen of my teeth—'

'Stop, stop!' said Fliss, laughing. 'You're saying all your lines without waiting for your cues!'

Mari waved a hand airily. 'Oh, cues. I know those too.' She took a breath. 'How now? Who calls? Your mother. Madam, I am here. What is your will? This is the matter . . . and so on and so on.'

'I'm sure Shakespeare didn't write "and so on and so on",' said Fliss, grinning.

Victoria was open-mouthed. 'How do you do that? How do you know everyone's lines, not just your own?'

Mari shrugged at the sky. 'Dunno. It just happens. Photographic memory, I guess.'

'I wish I could do that. Why don't the lines just stay in my head too?'

'Mari's always been good at learning stuff off by heart,' said Fliss. 'Remember that assembly we had to do at the last minute? Everyone kept looking at Mari because she was the only one who could remember what was supposed to happen next.'

'It's a burden as well as a blessing,' said Mari dramatically.

'I don't see how,' said Victoria. 'I'd give my right arm to be able to remember things that easily. I can't even remember where I've left my front-door key half the time.' Mari snorted. 'No, it's true!' insisted Victoria. 'Yesterday I went out for rehearsal and when I got back I couldn't get into the house because I'd left the key on the kitchen table. I could even *see* the thing from the back door!'

'What did you do?' asked Fliss, amused.

'Had to get Sonja up, didn't I?' said Victoria. 'Honestly, I don't know why she wanted to be an au pair. She spends most of the day sleeping, I think. And then she's on the internet all night, talking to her friends in goodness-knows-where.'

'Wish we had an au pair,' said Mari enviously. 'I have to do all the washing and cleaning at home.'

'She doesn't do it very well,' said Victoria. 'Mum's always complaining about her.'

'Shouldn't you be going for your fitting soon?' asked Fliss suddenly.

Victoria sat bolt upright. 'Oh God! What's the time?'

'Quarter to.'

Victoria leaped to her feet. 'She's going to kill me! I was meant to be in at half past! See you in a minute!' She dashed into the building.

Mari lay back and closed her eyes. 'This is the life,' she said contentedly.

Fliss lay back too and smiled. 'It's pretty good, isn't it?'

'When the weather's like this, I almost feel sorry we spend so much time in rehearsals indoors,' said Mari. 'Don't get me wrong, I love acting. And this play is going to be awesome. But it takes up a lot of lazing-around time.'

Fliss laughed. 'You seem to be fitting in as much as possible.'

'I'd do more of nothing if I could,' said Mari drily. 'Though my mum's pleased I'm in the play because it gets me out of the house.'

'I like having something to work on,' mused Fliss. 'I like having something to think about; get excited about.'

Mari rolled over onto one arm and looked at Fliss. 'Are we talking about the play or about Tom?'

Fliss felt that strange pain that always shot through

her when she heard his name, but she kept her expression neutral. 'I don't know what you mean. He's still going out with Samantha.' She tried to sound as though she didn't care. 'It's got nothing to do with me.'

'Yeah, right.' Mari snorted. 'You can't fool me.'

'No, really.' Fliss rolled onto her side so she could face Mari. 'I've been thinking about what you said. When he asked me out and I said no. You said maybe it was because my subconscious was trying to tell me we weren't meant to be together.'

'You don't want to listen to me!' said Mari in alarm. 'I was just trying to make you feel better!'

'And you did,' said Fliss, smiling. 'I'm OK with it. There's no point wasting my time thinking about him. And look at it this way . . .' She settled herself more comfortably on one arm. 'If he goes for girls like Samantha, then he wouldn't suit me anyway. We are so totally different.'

'Yeah,' agreed Mari, 'you're nice and she's a—'

'Model,' said Fliss firmly. 'She's tall, I'm short.'

'Petite.'

'She's blonde and I'm brunette. She's glamorous and I'm not.' Fliss shook her head. 'We couldn't be more different. So if there's something about

Samantha he really likes – then he wouldn't like me.'

Mari was staring at her. 'You've got this all worked out, haven't you? Well, have you thought about the text thing?'

Fliss looked puzzled. 'What do you mean?'

'You know when he got that text from her in rehearsal? Did you see him text her back?' asked Mari. 'Have you *ever* seen him text or ring her?'

'No, but that doesn't mean—'

'What it *does* mean,' interrupted Mari, 'is that she's doing all the running. She's got her claws into Tom and she's hanging onto him. I bet he's not even really that interested.'

'You said he looked pretty interested when you saw them snogging,' contradicted Fliss.

'That was ages ago,' said Mari.

'But they're still going *out*, Mari. You can't get away from that.' Fliss sighed. 'I know you're trying to be helpful, but really, it would be easier if we didn't talk about him.' Mari hesitated. '*Please*,' said Fliss.

Mari's face relaxed into a smile. 'Of course. Let's talk about something else instead. How about the likelihood of Victoria's costume being all black again?'

'Sssh!' Fliss looked up. 'Here she comes!'

Victoria looked mutinous. 'Typical,' she was muttering. 'Just typical.'

'You OK?' asked Mari innocently.

'Black!' said Victoria furiously. 'Black top, black skirt, black tights, black shoes. Honestly! You'd have thought they could spare me some kind of tunic. But no! And I have to get all the stuff myself. I don't *own* a black skirt!'

Fliss and Mari caught each other's eye and burst out giggling.

'What's so funny?' demanded Victoria.

'Mari just said she bet your costume would be all black again,' said Fliss, trying to stop laughing.

'Well that's hilarious,' said Victoria sarcastically. 'I'm so pleased you find it so *amusing*.'

'Sorry,' said Fliss, giving Mari a nudge. 'I know you wanted something nice this time.'

'It's only because I had all blacks last time,' said Victoria. 'That's the trouble with being the narrator, or the chorus, or somebody who isn't a real character. They think you don't need a costume.' She sat down with a thump. 'I've seen yours,' she added to Fliss. Her face looked wistful. 'It's so pretty. I wish I had something like that.'

'Does Mrs Carstairs want me yet?' asked Mari.

Victoria nodded. 'She's running a bit late. She said would you both go in together so she can do you at the same time.'

Fliss gathered up her bag. 'We'd better go,' she told Mari. Now that both Sarah and Victoria had mentioned her costume, she felt excited about seeing it for herself.

'Really sorry,' said Mari to Victoria, but she spoiled the sincerity by snorting with laughter.

'Yes, ha ha,' said Victoria. 'I just hope your costume is even worse.'

Fliss and Mari hurried indoors. Fliss felt some relief at getting in out of the hot sun, but that relief evaporated when they tramped down to the basement. The temperature rose with every step down, and when she opened the door to the costume store they were hit by a wave of heat.

The room was stuffed full to bursting with costumes of every colour and material possible. Rails of costumes on hangers took up most of the space, whilst pairs of Victorian boots mingled with ballet pumps and plimsolls on the floor. Perched on top of the rails and in the cupboards lining the walls were top hats, feather boas, bonnets, lace fans, gloves, fake-fur stoles, alongside all sorts of unidentifiable objects. 'Whoa,' said Mari. 'There's twice as much stuff as the last time I was in here.'

Fliss felt a tingle of excitement. It might have been shabby and cramped, but she felt as though this room was where the magic of performance began.

'No windows in here,' called a voice. Mrs Carstairs was on her knees underneath a clothing rail, retrieving a dress that had fallen on the floor. 'Sorry it's so hot.'

Mari wrinkled her nose. 'It's not just the heat . . .'

Fliss knew what she meant. There was a strong smell of − what? Sweat? Dust? Feet? It wasn't pleasant, at any rate. But Mrs Carstairs was crawling out from the rail and Fliss remembered what Sarah had said. 'Don't mention the smell,' she whispered to Mari.

Mrs Carstairs stood up and brushed the greying hair out of her eyes. She was a plump woman, with a permanently harassed look. 'I'm sorry, we're running a bit behind. Fliss, I'll just pull out your three costumes . . .' She clattered some hangers together.

'Three?' asked Fliss in some surprise.

'Yes,' said Mrs Carstairs. 'You can't wear the same

dress all the way through. Unfortunately for me. You've got a simple dress for most of your scenes . . .' She lifted out something long and silky, made of dark red fabric. 'You die in this one too,' she added matter-of-factly. 'Then you've got a nightdress . . .' This one was more like a tent of white cotton. 'Not very authentic, I'm afraid. We couldn't get quite the right thing. If you make it with the real stuff, it doesn't last. Anyway. You can try them on in a minute. The one I really want to check is along here . . .' She rustled along the rack. 'This is the one we borrowed from the BBC.' She lifted it out almost reverently. 'And you must take special care of it. They're all dry-clean only.'

'Oh, Fliss,' said Mari in a whisper. 'It's beautiful.'

Fliss was speechless. The dress was a deep midnight blue. The skirts were full and made of velvet. The top part of the dress was a satiny fabric, with tiny pearls embroidered all over it in a diamond pattern. There were little puffed sleeves too, made of the same satin fabric.

'Come on then,' said Mrs Carstairs practically, 'let's get you into it.'

Quickly, Fliss took off her shorts and slipped into the dress. The back was open right to the waist. 'How does it do up?'

'It's a laced corset,' said Mrs Carstairs. She held up two ends of a piece of string. 'It takes some practice to do, but I'm expecting to be in the dressing room with you girls during the performance, so I should be able to do it up for you.' She began lacing the string through the little holes and pulling them tight.

'Oof!' Fliss gasped. 'Is it meant to be that tight?'

'Yes,' said Mrs Carstairs firmly. 'It can't jiggle around. Besides, it was the fashion. And it'll help you get into character. Juliet would have been taught how to stand properly. How to hold herself.'

'She wouldn't need to hold herself at all in this dress,' said Fliss, finding it harder and harder to breathe. 'It holds *you* up, not the other way around.'

'There,' said Mrs Carstairs, pulling the final loop tight and tying the strings at the back. 'Let's have a look at you.'

'She looks *gorgeous*,' said Mari enthusiastically.

Mrs Carstairs nodded critically. 'Yes, it's a good fit.'

Fliss wasn't sure she agreed with that. The dress felt far too tight for her liking, but then Mrs Carstairs pointed at a full-length mirror hanging on the wall. Fliss felt a thrill pass through her. She looked – well – like a princess. Her petite frame was enhanced by the corset, which pulled in her waist and gave her more shape. And the dark blue richness of the dress set off her dark hair and eyes perfectly. Fliss ran her fingers gently over her skirt, marvelling at its softness. Suddenly the tightness of the corset didn't matter any more.

'Good,' said Mrs Carstairs, though her voice had lost its sharp edge and there was a slight mistiness to her eyes as she looked at Fliss. 'That's a relief. Nothing to alter there.' She glanced down. 'Even the length is perfect.' She took a breath, and the harassed look was back in her face. 'Take it off then.'

Fliss felt rather disappointed to be wriggling out of the dress, but she consoled herself with the thought that she'd be able to wear it in re-hearsals soon. Her other two outfits fitted with room to spare, but Mrs Carstairs thought she could get away without altering them. 'It's good to have a bit of extra give here and there. Speaking of which . . .' She turned to Mari. 'Let me dig out your costume, Mari.'

Fliss had the nightdress over her head when she heard Mari gulp, so it wasn't until she had taken the costume off that she saw what had caused Mari's reaction.

'This is the Nurse's costume,' said Mrs Carstairs. She was holding up something that could only be described as a tent. It was a shapeless mass of brown and white fabric that didn't even seem to have recognizable sleeves. 'Arms up,' said Mrs Carstairs to Mari, who hadn't even taken off her strappy top and shorts. The voluminous material settled down over Mari, making her look like a small round cake with a head sticking out the top. She looked absolutely horrified.

Fliss wanted to laugh but she sensed Mari wouldn't respond well to this at all, so she bit her lip as hard as she could. 'Oh. My. God,' Mari mouthed when Mrs Carstairs's back was turned. 'I look like a Christmas pudding.'

'And here's the headscarf,' said Mrs Carstairs, producing a large white square which she tied around Mari's head like a nun's wimple.

'You are kidding,' said Mari in a strangled voice.

'What do you mean?' asked Mrs Carstairs, absorbed in her task. 'This is how the Nurse is traditionally seen, Mari. Your costume is from the BBC too, you know. We were lucky to get it.'

Mari didn't look as though she agreed. 'I'm drowning in it,' she said.

Mrs Carstairs stood back and looked her up and

down. 'Hmm,' she said. 'Yes. You are rather.' Mari looked relieved, but her face dropped when Mrs Carstairs said, 'We'll just have to find you some padding. Hang on a minute.' She opened a cupboard door and a whole box of vests and underwear toppled out. 'Oops. I do wish we had more *room* . . . Now, where did I put . . . ? Ah!' She turned round. 'Here it is.'

There was a stunned silence. Then Mari whispered, '*That?* You want me to wear . . . *that?*'

The laughter that had been bubbling in Fliss overflowed. She let out a gigantic snort and then collapsed into hysterical giggles.

'It's a perfectly practical solution,' said Mrs Carstairs, holding the enormous padded bra and looking a little annoyed. 'You're behaving like children. Fliss, if you've finished, you can get dressed and go.'

Fliss, almost crying with laughter, hastily pulled on her shorts. It would probably be best if she left, since Mari looked as though she was about to explode with anger. As she closed the door behind her, she heard Mrs Carstairs say to Mari, 'Right, let me show you how to put it on . . .'

♥

'I hate you,' said Mari to Fliss ten minutes later when she had rejoined the others on the lawn. 'You have three really gorgeous dresses and what do I have? A brown tent that makes me look like a giant dog poo!'

'How's the *bra?*' asked Victoria with a straight face, before her lip wobbled and she started to laugh.

'Oh, *very* funny.' Mari glared. 'Your black outfit doesn't sound so bad now, does it?'

'I can't wait to see you in it,' said Victoria.

'Yeah, yeah, you and the rest of the cast,' grumbled Mari. 'It makes me look like some dumpy old woman. Sean came in just as I was finishing my fitting and he thought I *was* Mrs Carstairs for a minute.'

'He didn't!' giggled Fliss. 'What happened?'

'Started saying did she have anything that wouldn't make his legs look too skinny and that he didn't want lace because it was girly.'

Victoria was nearly hysterical with laughter. 'What did you say?' she gasped.

'Told him all the boys were wearing tights and that lace ruffs were compulsory for the time period,' said Mari, a half-smile on her lips. 'Then he realized I wasn't Mrs Carstairs at all.'

'Did he look embarrassed?' asked Fliss. 'I wouldn't think so. Sean's not the type.'

'Actually, he did look a bit red,' said Mari. 'Specially when he saw my enormous – ahem – you know. *Padded bra*.' She rolled her eyes.

Victoria giggled again. 'He didn't ask to feel it?'

'Ew no!' said Mari. Then she added, 'But I did offer to let him borrow it. The bra, I mean. In case he was going to any fancy dress parties soon. He said he'd think about it.'

'I think Sean fancies you,' said Fliss unexpectedly. The other two looked up, startled. 'No, really. He's normally kind of loud and silly, but he goes all quiet if he has to talk to you, Mari. Hadn't you noticed?'

'No,' said Mari, snorting in disbelief. 'You're making it up.'

Victoria frowned. 'She's not, you know. I hadn't really thought about it, but she's right. He does get sort of quiet and respectful if you say something. It's weird, since you'd think he'd get louder if he wanted you to notice him.'

Mari was still looking sceptical. 'Sean? Fancy me?'

'He's quite nice,' said Fliss. 'Underneath all that show-off act. He was really sweet to me in *Match Girl* when we had to do that duet.'

'You'd make a good couple,' said Victoria to Mari. 'I think he's just your type.'

Mari went pink. 'I'm sure he doesn't fancy me. You two are just being evil.'

'See what it's like to have people matchmaking you all the time?' said Fliss maliciously.

'Well, there's an easy way to find out,' said Mari decisively. 'I'll just ask him.'

Victoria's mouth dropped open so wide she nearly fell over. 'You'll *what*?'

'I'll ask him.' Mari shrugged. 'Then I'll know, won't I?'

'But you can't do that!' said Fliss, staring.

'Why not?'

'Because – but – aren't you—' Fliss spluttered. 'Wouldn't you be embarrassed?'

'Why should I?' Mari looked at her. 'He's the one who fancies *me*, you said.'

'Yes, but . . .' Fliss trailed off.

'She's bluffing,' said Victoria suddenly. 'She wouldn't really do it.'

Mari raised her eyebrows. 'Oh, wouldn't I?'

'Hang on, hang on,' interrupted Fliss. 'Aren't we missing the point here?'

'What do you mean?'

'Well, do you fancy *him*, Mari? I mean, if he says he

does fancy you, what are you going to do about it? Do you like him?'

Mari seemed temporarily stumped. 'I don't know. He's all right, I suppose. A bit tall for me.'

'You could stand on a box to kiss him,' suggested Victoria.

'Oh thank you, that's very helpful,' said Mari sarcastically.

Fliss clapped her hands. 'This is fab. Go on, Mari, ask him if he fancies you.'

'I'm going to.'

'And if he says yes, then you can ask him out!'

'Oooh!' said Victoria, her eyes shining. 'Mari's got a boyfriend, Mari's got a boyfriend!'

'What if he says no?' asked Mari, waggling her finger at Victoria. 'You haven't thought of that one, have you?'

'But he likes you,' said Fliss. 'I'm sure.'

'Yes, *but*, Miss Matchmaking Felicity, even if he does, he might not actually *admit* it, might he? I mean mightn't he? Or something.'

'She's got a point,' said Victoria. 'Boys never like admitting they fancy someone.'

'Then Mari will just have to wear her padded bra all the time until he does fancy her,' said Fliss solemnly.

There was a pause, and all three of them burst out laughing. 'Well, I'll tell you what, Fliss,' said Mari, between giggles. 'If you want to get Tom's attention, I'll let you borrow it. That's one thing Samantha definitely doesn't have – a forty double D chest!'

Chapter 11

meant for each other

Fliss shivered slightly in her red dress. It might have been the height of summer, but there was a chilly breeze today.

'You've got goosebumps,' said Mari, who was standing next to her. 'You all right?'

'Just a bit cold,' said Fliss, rubbing her arms. 'I'm sure when I get started I'll warm up. And this costume is thinner than it looks.'

'I guess we had to do a run-through outside at some point,' said Mari. 'It's good they let us try out the costumes too. And the final dress rehearsal is only six days away!' She gulped.

Fliss nodded. 'It was time we got on the set. I'm fed up of pretending to be standing on a balcony. It's great to see the real thing.' She looked around. 'It's weird to be doing a proper run-through outside with everyone though. I'd almost forgotten there were other people in the play, I've been so wrapped up in my scenes! I can't wait to see the sword fights.'

'Thank goodness Victoria didn't get a sword after all,' said Mari. 'Have you seen them practising? Those swords are scary!'

The whole cast was gathered in the town park. The park was large, with a long sweeping lawn surrounded by beautifully arranged flowerbeds. There was a wooded area, a wooden bandstand in need of redecorating, and a boating lake. The *Romeo and Juliet* set had been built at one end of the lawn, with an imposing frontage and beautifully painted balcony. There were even billowing curtains in the windows. Before they had got into costume, Candy had shown everyone around the set. The balcony was accessed by a ladder behind the stage, and there were also two trapdoors in the raised wooden floor. Three hidden exits led through the flowerbeds to the wooded area, which hid two large tents that acted as dressing rooms – one for the girls and one for the boys. There was even a small gazebo that housed five musicians, who were to accompany the scene changes.

'This is way more impressive than *Match Girl*,' said Mari. 'I mean, this is proper staging and everything.' She took a step forward and then realized someone was standing on her costume. 'Doug, get off my dress.'

A short boy with glasses grinned. 'Sorry, Mrs Carstairs.'

Mari made an exasperated noise. 'Will you all stop doing that! It's not funny any more!'

Fliss hid a smile. Sean had told everyone about Mari's amplified underclothing, and how he had mistaken her for the costume lady. Since then, several members of the cast had taken to calling Mari 'Mrs Carstairs', much to her annoyance.

Mari glared at Doug until he moved. Then she nodded towards the balcony. 'You sure you're going to be safe up there, Fliss?'

'Oh yes,' said Fliss. 'I've been up there a couple of times now. Candy said I should try going up and down to make sure I was really comfortable with it. She showed me how to hold the ladder properly – at the sides, not on the rungs. It makes everything much easier, and I can hold my skirt up at the same time. It all feels very solid, and actually there's a bit more space at the top than I was expecting. Though the balcony rail is quite low.'

'Just don't go headlong over the top,' said Mari. 'That would put a dampener on the whole thing.' She brightened. 'Though maybe Tom could catch you?'

Fliss waved a hand airily. 'I am so over him,' she declared. 'He's still going out with Samantha. It's never going to happen for me. It's fine.' *Maybe if I keep saying it*, she thought, *I'll believe it too*.

'Yeah, right,' muttered Mari. 'Methinks the lady doth protest too much.'

The music started up, and the cast behind the set fell silent. Fliss felt a familiar jolt of excitement. She knew it wasn't the real thing – opening night was still a week away – but there was something about the magic of theatre that got to her every time. It was like a tiny thrill that ran up and down her back and made her goosebumps even worse. Mari mistook her arm-rubbing as another sign she was cold. 'Here,' she said, holding out her costume like a tent, 'share this. There's enough of it to go round.'

Fliss and Mari saw Victoria run onto the stage with the other narrators, and heard her begin the famous lines: 'Two households, both alike in dignity . . .'

'Ssh!' said Samantha, glaring at them, even though they hadn't been talking. Mari threw her a disgusted look. Samantha was dressed head-to-toe in black and was carrying a small radio so that she could talk to Candy from backstage. She also had a pencil-thin torch stuck in one back pocket and a hairbrush in the other. Her glossy blonde hair was neatly caught into a long plait. As the opening speech went on, she bit one of her nails and began to look bored.

Fliss's first scene went well, though she was surprised how difficult it was to speak loudly. It was almost as though any sound she made just disappeared into the air. She was also rather distracted when a plane flew low overhead.

After their scene, Mari and Fliss made their way into the dressing tent. 'I haven't got long,' said Fliss, pulling her red dress over her head. 'I'm meant to be back in a minute for the party scene.' Mrs Carstairs bustled over and started lacing her into the blue dress.

'Did you hear that plane?' said Mari. 'I hope that doesn't happen on the night.'

'Day,' said Mrs Carstairs. 'Afternoon performance.' She pulled the laces tight.

Mari rolled her eyes. Fliss didn't try to explain how the performance was always referred to as 'on the night' even when it wasn't night-time. She took an experimental breath and felt the corset press against her. 'I was more worried about my voice,' she admitted.

'Your voice?'

'Didn't it sound really thin and reedy to you?'

Mari frowned. 'No, I don't think so. You sound the same to me. Bit quieter maybe.'

'That's the problem,' said Fliss. 'It's almost like—'

Samantha came rustling through the bushes. 'Fliss!' she snapped. 'You're on!'

'I am?' Fliss gasped. Mrs Carstairs made a noise of annoyance and tied the laces in double-quick time. Fliss ran back to the stage, but Mercutio was still in the middle of his Queen Mab speech. She felt annoyed. Samantha had made her panic for no reason. It wasn't even her cue yet!

There wasn't any point heading back to the tent. She only had a minute or two before she had to be on stage. Fliss let her eyes wander over the back of the set. It really was a wonderfully put-together balcony. It must have taken hours to paint. Fliss wondered who Candy had persuaded to do it. Candy seemed to have friends in every theatrical company in the county. From the stage Fliss could hear Tom interrupting Mercutio, saying 'Peace, peace, Mercutio, peace!' Her stomach flipped. Even just hearing his voice made her feel funny! Fliss twisted her fingers together in annoyance. She was really trying to forget him. There was no point mooning over a boy who was already taken. And if Tom was attracted to girls like Samantha, then he'd never notice her anyway. It was just impossible!

A low rumble overhead made Fliss look up, frowning, but it wasn't a plane this time. The sky was turning grey. She hoped the rain would hold off until they finished the play.

Mari came stumbling through the undergrowth, saying a rude word as her long skirts tripped her up. 'Come on,' she said, 'didn't you hear the cue?'

Fliss blinked, startled, and realized the music for the party scene had just started. She had been thinking about Tom again – why did he do this to her? Why was he so different from the other boys? And it wasn't even as though he was making life difficult for her. In their most recent rehearsals he couldn't have been nicer to her! Though, Fliss reflected, in some ways that just made things harder, not easier. Mari took her hand and tugged her onto the stage, and Fliss dragged her mind back to the play. She must concentrate!

By the end of the party scene, the clouds were definitely gathering, and Fliss wasn't the only one to be looking anxiously up at the sky. Mari nudged her. 'Ready to make a run for it if the heavens open?'

'Where to?' whispered Fliss. 'We can't all fit in the tents, can we?'

'Bandstand,' said Mari. 'The one round the corner. It's closer than the tents, and has a better roof. If the wind gets up, those tents will blow away. I'm heading for the bandstand if it does rain.'

Fliss nodded. 'Good idea.'

The rehearsal was going well. There were some minor slip-ups when people forgot their lines. Sean came on from the wrong side twice and stopped in confusion. Mari pointed him in the right direction and he thanked her, blushing. Fliss nudged her. 'Asked him yet?'

'I'm picking my moment, OK?' said Mari with a grin.

By the end of the scene in which Mercutio and Tybalt were killed, a few drops of rain were starting to fall. Fliss could see Candy sitting in a plastic chair out front, anxiously looking at her watch. Candy wouldn't want to get all the costumes wet, Fliss supposed, but on the other hand they would only have one other run-through before the dress rehearsal the following Friday. There were still some problems that needed sorting. Candy wouldn't want to abandon the rehearsal unless absolutely necessary . . .

The rain stopped and everyone breathed a sigh of relief. Maybe they would get through the whole thing after all?

But it was not to be. Fliss and Tom were on stage, performing Act III Scene 5. Fliss had just begun her speech, 'Wilt thou be gone? It is not yet near day,' when the whole sky seemed to empty itself all at once. Enormous raindrops splattered the stage, drenching it in seconds. Fliss found herself wet through before she had even realized it was raining. In the audience, Candy abandoned her chair and ran for it. 'Get under cover!' she called. Fliss found it hard even to see Tom, the rain was so heavy.

'Let's go!' yelled Tom, and headed for one of the exits.

'No!' shouted Fliss. 'Bandstand!' She jabbed her arm towards it. 'More room!'

Tom hesitated for a moment, then nodded, and the two of them dashed off the stage and round the flowerbeds to the large wooden bandstand. The rain was thumping down on the metal roof, but there was little wind, so the middle of the bandstand floor was perfectly dry. Tom and Fliss ran up the steps and stopped, shivering, in the middle of the floor. All the way round them, water thundered down in sheets, almost as though the bandstand had walls after all. The noise from the rain on the roof was terrific.

Fliss looked around, but there was no sign of Mari.

In fact, there was no sign of anyone else at all. 'Where are the others?' she yelled to Tom.

Streams of water were running down the sides of his face from his flattened dark curls. He rubbed his nose with a damp sleeve. 'No idea!' he yelled back. 'Maybe they're all in the tents, like I suggested!'

Fliss felt guilty. 'Sorry!' she shouted. 'I thought this would be a better place to shelter.'

Tom shrugged and looked out across the park. Fliss glanced out too and felt quite astonished at the sight. The rain was so heavy, it was washing away parts of the flowerbeds before their eyes. Mud streamed across the tarmac paths, and the carefully planted flowers were being crushed under the weight of rain. Fliss looked automatically towards the stage set, but it couldn't be seen from the bandstand. She hoped it would stand up all right. The curtains at the windows would be completely sodden, of course, but hopefully the rest of the set would dry out eventually.

'Guess that means the rehearsal's over,' Tom called to her.

'What?'

'I said, guess the rehearsal's over then,' he shouted again.

'Oh.' Fliss nodded. 'Yes.' A chill swept over her. Just her luck she was in the flimsy nightdress and not the heavy velvet party costume! In fact . . . Fliss glanced down in quick panic but was relieved to see that her wet nightdress had not become see-through. Nevertheless, it was clinging to her very closely, and she crossed her arms in a vain attempt to cover herself up a bit.

'You OK?' Tom asked. The rain had eased slightly, and they could at least hear themselves think. 'Are you cold?'

'A bit,' admitted Fliss. A sudden flash lit the sky and she jumped.

'It's only lightning,' said Tom.

'Yeah, and we're only under a metal roof,' snapped Fliss, trying to stop her teeth from chattering.

Tom looked puzzled, but suddenly he remembered. 'You're scared of thunderstorms,' he said.

'No need to rub it in.'

Tom laughed. 'You're OK standing on a wooden floor. Just don't touch the metal posts, that's all.'

She glared at him.

'I'm joking,' he said. 'I'm sure we'll be fine. Unless you want to make a run for it?'

Fliss looked out at the park, but at that moment the thunder crashed overhead, making the floor tremble beneath them. She let out an involuntary yelp.

In a couple of steps, Tom was standing next to her. 'It's OK, Fliss. Don't panic.'

'I hate thunder,' said Fliss.

'What?' He bent closer to hear her.

'I hate thunder! And lightning! People die from being hit by lightning, you know!' There was another flash and Fliss flinched.

'Here,' said Tom, and he put his arms around her as though it were the most natural thing in the world. 'It's all right. It'll be over soon.'

There was another huge crash, and Fliss felt like she wanted to cry. 'It just gets right inside me – you know, the noise. I hate it.'

Tom's arms tightened around her. 'It won't last long.' He was silent for a moment and then said, 'You're scared of quite a lot of things, aren't you?'

'What do you mean?' Fliss was momentarily distracted. 'What sorts of things?'

Tom gave a half-shrug. 'I don't know. Confrontation. People who speak up for themselves. Loud noises. It seems weird how on stage you know exactly what you're doing, but off-stage you're a bit like – well – a mouse.'

Fliss bit her lip. 'It's not that I'm scared,' she objected.

'I just don't like people getting cross. Or angry. Or upset.'

'You'd like everyone to be happy and get on with each other all the time,' suggested Tom. He removed a strand of Fliss's hair from her face and tucked it behind her ear.

'What's wrong with that?' Fliss tried to sound indignant, but what he had just done with her hair made her feel strange. It was such an intimate gesture. Her ear tingled from where his hand had brushed it. She quickly reached to tuck all other strands of her hair out of the way, which was difficult with his arms still around her.

'People don't get on all the time though, do they?' said Tom. He stared down at her. 'Some people just don't – click. And then there are others who . . .' He trailed off.

Fliss couldn't move. His eyes were holding hers, and she suddenly noticed what a very deep blue they were. Like looking into the sea on a summer's day . . .

'Are you still cold?' asked Tom softly. 'You're trembling.'

Fliss opened her mouth to reply but no words came out. Tom brushed another hair away from her face, and the back of his hand stroked her cheek. 'There are others . . .' he whispered, 'who just seem . . . meant for each other.'

Fliss felt a strange falling sensation – almost as though the ground were melting under her feet. The rain was still coming down, but it was a background shushing noise now, a gentle musical sound. Tom's face swam before her, and without thinking, she placed her hands on his chest. He felt so warm. So strong. *Meant for each other*, he'd said. Fliss's head swam in that deep blue sea. Tom leaned towards her. *Meant for each other* . . .

'What about Samantha?' Fliss whispered, her lips barely moving.

Tom stopped, his face millimetres from hers. 'What?'

'Samantha.' Fliss blinked, and a cold wave swept through her. 'You're going out with Samantha.'

Time stopped for a moment. Tom and Fliss stared at each other. A thousand thoughts were whirling through Fliss's head. He was going out with Samantha. So why was he trying to kiss her? *Just say*, she thought, *just tell me Samantha means nothing. Tell me you're going to go out with me instead. Tell me!*

Tom took a step back, and his arms dropped to his sides. He looked confused. 'I – uh . . .' he said. 'Yes. I'm going out with Samantha.'

In an awful moment, Fliss thought she was going to cry. It was as though the ground had come crashing back up to meet her feet, and she actually staggered. Her head felt dizzy with shock. He had been about to kiss her! Why had she blurted out that thing about Samantha? Was she a complete idiot?

Tom had turned away and was staring at the rain. An awkward silence descended, and Fliss felt the chill of the rain on her body again now that Tom's arms were no longer around her. 'It's stopping,' said Tom flatly. 'We'd better get back.'

Fliss blinked furiously and rubbed her eyes. 'All right,' she said in what she hoped was a normal voice.

Tom didn't glance back at her before he stepped down to the grass and began heading for the tents. Fliss followed miserably, trying to hold back the tears. She'd done it again! For the second time she'd messed everything up!

As they rounded the corner, Fliss saw the one person she least wanted to. Samantha was standing outside the tent, peering towards them. 'Tom!' she cried as he approached. 'Thank goodness! Where have you been?' Then she caught sight of Fliss, following Tom, and her face turned to stone. 'Have you been with *her*?' she said coldly.

'Leave it, OK?' said Tom in a tired voice. He went to walk past her, but Samantha grabbed his arm.

'No way,' she hissed. 'Where were you two? Why didn't you go with everyone else?'

Fliss wanted nothing more than to get into the tent and out of her wet costume, but Samantha was blocking her way. Miserably, she stood on the wet grass, feeling her feet slip and squeak inside her ballet pumps.

'Look, there's nothing to worry about,' said Tom to Samantha. 'We went to the bandstand. When it stopped raining we came back. End of story. OK?'

Samantha hesitated, but then she dropped his arm. 'Well, why didn't you say so?' she said brightly, and leaned forward to kiss him. Tom turned his face so that the kiss landed on his cheek.

'I've got to get changed,' he said abruptly, and walked off towards the boys' dressing tent.

Samantha's eyes narrowed as she turned to look at Fliss. 'I don't know what you think you're playing at,' she said in a dangerous voice, 'but don't you dare try to steal my boyfriend. Or you'll be sorry.'

Fliss felt drained of all energy, so she simply nodded. Samantha stared at her once more before turning on her heel and marching off, calling over her shoulder,

'You'll have to take that costume home and dry it yourself.'

Mari and Victoria came bursting out of the bushes. 'You OK? My goodness, you're like a drowned rat! Where have you been?'

Fliss shook her head. 'The bandstand.'

Mari looked curious. 'On your own?'

'No,' said Fliss unwillingly. 'Tom was there.'

Mari and Victoria exchanged a look. 'You and Tom in the bandstand – just you?' said Victoria. 'How romantic!'

'It wasn't romantic at all,' snapped Fliss. She suddenly wanted to go home and climb into bed and not talk to anyone at all. Even her best friends.

Mari peered at her. 'What happened? Have you been crying?'

'I'm fine,' said Fliss. 'Nothing happened.' *Which is true*, she thought. *It would have done, if I hadn't opened my big stupid mouth. He would have kissed me. Properly. Not as Juliet – as Fliss. But that would have been wrong, wouldn't it? He's going out with someone else!* She felt absurdly angry. How dare he put her in that situation!

The sky was clearing but the air was still chilly. Fliss's nightdress clung to her, making her colder by the minute. 'We've got to get you warmed up,' said

Victoria, noticing Fliss shivering. 'Come on, we'll look after you.'

The two of them put their arms around Fliss and helped her back to the tent. At the doorway, Fliss couldn't help looking back at the clearing. But Tom and Samantha were long gone.

Chapter 12

you'll get over it

Fliss felt cold for a long time that night, even though Jeanette had made her a hot-water bottle, and she was wearing thick socks. She lay back and stared at the ceiling. All she could see was Tom's face. His eyes, drawing her in. His hand, brushing the hair away from her cheek.

And then she heard her own voice, asking about Samantha. Ruining the moment – spoiling her chance. Two more seconds and she would have had her very first kiss. Not a pretend one on the stage. A real kiss meant for her, Felicity Richards. But she had to go and mess it all up. Maybe if Tom had kissed her there, in the rain, he might have realized how she felt about him. How she still felt, despite trying to ignore her feelings. And he might have decided to split up with Samantha . . . but how would Fliss have felt about that? She didn't want to be responsible for them breaking up, did she? No. He was taken.

He was someone else's boyfriend. It was wrong to go behind their backs, wasn't it? Even if that person was Samantha. It would still be wrong to cheat with her boyfriend.

Fliss felt all mixed up in the head. Why did things have to be so complicated? And why, even though she knew she'd done the right thing, did she wish she hadn't?

♥

'Something's going on,' Jeanette said four days later. She looked at her daughter with a frown. 'I've never seen you this miserable. It's not good for you. You usually like being in plays. You get excited. Over-happy. Not like this.' She sighed as she cleared the kitchen table. 'And you're not eating properly. You've got to eat, Felicity. At least have some fruit for pudding.'

Fliss glanced at the two ancient apples and the wrinkled orange in the basket. 'No thanks.'

'Some yoghurt then.'

Fliss shook her head. Jeanette sighed. 'Now listen, love, don't get angry with me, but . . . well, have you thought about pulling out of the play?'

Fliss gave her mother a look.

179

Jeanette held up her hands. 'I know, I know, I don't understand, you can't possibly do that, no one can do your part, blah blah. But sweetie, if you were hit by a bus and were in hospital, they'd have to manage without you, wouldn't they? Someone else could do your lines.' Fliss rolled her eyes. 'I'm just *saying*,' said Jeanette, her voice sharpening, 'that it's not the end of the world. This play is making you unhappy. I don't know what happened the other night, but obviously it was something big. And since you won't tell me, I'm just guessing in the dark here.' Jeanette was sounding more annoyed by the minute. 'You've been up and down more in the past few weeks than you have in the past few years.'

'Maybe it's because I'm a teenager,' muttered Fliss rebelliously. 'Aren't you going to mention hormones?'

Jeanette sat down. 'Don't take that tone with me. I'm only trying to help. And as a matter of fact, Vivienne did mention hormone levels only yesterday.' She caught her daughter's accusing stare. 'I was worried,' she said defensively. 'I rang Vivienne to see if she had any advice. She said Sofie went through something very similar at your age. But then she put her on starflower and evening primrose oil and everything went back to normal.'

'I don't need vitamin tablets,' said Fliss, exasperated.

'Everyone needs vitamin tablets,' said Jeanette, who took three different sorts herself every morning. 'Especially if you're not eating a balanced diet,' she added pointedly.

'All right!' snapped Fliss. 'I'll eat a yoghurt, OK?'

Jeanette sighed. 'It's not just the eating, Felicity. You're so quiet – even quieter than normal. Why can't you tell me what's happened?'

'You wouldn't understand.'

'I might.' Jeanette put her hand over her daughter's. 'I was young once myself, you know. It wasn't that long ago.'

'When you were young,' said Fliss, 'they didn't even have the internet.'

'No,' agreed Jeanette, 'we talked to each other instead.'

Fliss bit her lip. 'All right. But you mustn't laugh.'

Jeanette nodded.

'There's this boy . . .' Fliss glanced up at her mum to see how she would react to this, but Jeanette's face remained impassive. 'You remember? The one we talked about before . . . I really like him. But he's going out with someone else.'

Jeanette smiled in relief. 'Oh, is that all!' She patted

Fliss's hand. 'I thought it was something serious! Sweetie, everyone gets crushes at your age.'

'It's not a crush!'

'And you'll get over it,' continued Jeanette. 'Is this the boy in the play? Tom something?'

Fliss nodded, dumbstruck. Her mother wasn't even trying to understand!

'Sweetheart,' said Jeanette, 'I know how intense it can feel. Like he's the only boy in the world for you. Like your life is going to fall apart if you can't be with him. But, darling' – she leaned forward and looked sympathetic – 'it's only another three days to the performance. The best way to get over someone is not to see them any more. Believe me, I know. After this weekend, you won't see him again, will you? So it'll stop hurting.' She smiled. 'And I bet by the time you get to the Christmas play, you'll have forgotten all about him.'

Fliss snatched her hand away and stood up so quickly her chair rocked violently. 'Stop talking to me as though I'm a child!'

Jeanette's jaw dropped. 'I beg your pardon?'

Fliss felt anger sweep through her – anger built on hurt and incomprehension. 'You don't even know how I feel! You have no idea!'

Her mother lifted her eyebrows. 'I do remember what it's like to be a teenager.'

'Maybe what it was like when *you* were a teenager, Mum.' Fliss felt hot with frustration. 'That was a long time ago.'

'Not that long,' said Jeanette sharply. She was astonished. Her little Fliss, answering back!

'And that was *you*, Mum, not me! You've said yourself how different we are! So stop patronizing me by saying you know how I feel!'

Jeanette's expression darkened. 'Now, hang on a minute . . .'

'You have *no* idea how much this play means to me. You think it's just silly nonsense. You've complained about it enough! But I love it, Mum, I love it more than *anything*. And you don't know the first thing about it! So how can you sit there and tell me that everything will be fine after the weekend? You don't know what you're talking about!'

'That's enough,' snapped Jeanette, getting to her feet. Fliss stopped, her face burning and her throat aching. 'Don't you dare speak to me like that! I'm fed up with the whole thing. I wish you'd never signed up for that play. Since you've been rehearsing, you've been moody and rude. Up and down all the time.'

Fliss clenched her fists at the injustice of this. When had she been rude? Jeanette was making it up!

'Especially the last few days,' Jeanette went on. 'You won't talk to me and you spend all your time in your room. You're not the only one who lives here, and I'm fed up with your mood swings. You're draining all the good energy out of the air. Every time I come into a room, I can feel your black mood. It's not good for either of us.'

'What are you talking about?' Fliss cried. 'Why are you spouting this rubbish at me? Good energy in the *air*? Come *on*, Mum, you know it's a load of tosh! It's just the sort of thing Vivienne would say!'

Jeanette's mouth dropped open. 'Vivienne talks a lot of sense!' she spluttered.

'No, she doesn't, Mum, she's a fake and you know it.' All the things she'd been bottling up suddenly came pouring out of Fliss. 'Why do you even have her round? She just looks down on you – on everything about us. Our house, the way we live – even the way I do my hair!'

'She does *not* look down on us,' said Jeanette, her face slowly turning beetroot. 'She's a good friend. She's given me a lot of good advice over the years.'

'Like what?' asked Fliss. 'What has she ever said that has made our lives even the slightest bit better?' Jeanette was speechless. 'You see? She just comes and tells you stuff because she knows you'll lap it up and it makes her feel all superior. She probably goes home and laughs about it afterwards!'

Jeanette's lip trembled. 'She's been a good friend,' she said, tears starting in her eyes. 'You don't know. When your dad . . . after all that, she was good to me. She was the only one who stuck by me.' Her voice suddenly rose, shrill and sharp. 'You have no idea what I went through! All alone! No one to look out for me!'

'You said you stayed with your parents.' Fliss's anger was subsiding. Her mother looked so upset and pathetic.

'Yes, but every single day, I felt like a stranger in their house. Mum said I was an idiot. She was so rude about Rob – about your father. She kept saying if only we could turn back the clock, but it was too late.' Jeanette turned miserable eyes on her daughter. 'You might think that Vivienne is stuck up,' she said quietly, 'but she's been more faithful to me than my own family. So don't you dare criticize her again.'

Fliss felt cold. Jeanette had never spoken to her like this before. But then she'd never dared argue until now. Her mother looked tired; broken. Fliss's heart ached for her. 'I'm sorry,' she said in a whisper.

Jeanette nodded. Her eyes no longer looked

unhappy. Now they looked hard, like stone. 'Do what you like,' she said. 'Do the play. Let this boy make you miserable. I don't care.' She turned and walked out of the room.

Fliss sat down heavily on a chair and tried not to cry.

♥

'Are you sure you're OK?' Mari asked anxiously for the sixth time. 'You just look so pale.'

The friends were getting ready for the Thursday run-through in the park. The tent was crowded with girls, but thankfully it hadn't rained since earlier in the day and there were clear skies over the stage. Candy had told them not to wear costumes, since they were too precious to risk getting wet again. 'You can wear them for the dress rehearsal tomorrow,' she said, 'but it'll cost us a fortune if any of them are damaged.' Fliss was a bit disappointed. The blue party dress in particular really helped her to get into the role of Juliet. She hoped the long skirt she was wearing would give her the same feeling.

Fliss glanced in her little hand mirror. Mari was right, she did look pale. 'I just didn't sleep too well. I'll put some blusher on.'

Victoria sighed. 'I wish you'd tell us what happened that day in the thunderstorm. Something did, didn't it?'

Fliss turned away to find her blusher. How could she admit that she had nearly kissed the boy of her dreams but ruined it all with one stupid comment? Mari and Victoria were shocked enough when she'd blown her chances of a date with Tom. What would they say if they knew she'd messed up a kiss too? It was too embarrassing. Instead, Fliss shrugged. 'Nothing happened.' Mari and Victoria looked unconvinced. 'It didn't! It might have – but it didn't. I just – I had an argument with my mum last night.'

Mari looked astonished. 'You *never* argue with your mum.'

'You never argue with *anyone*,' said Victoria.

'And now I know why,' said Fliss with a grimace. 'It was horrible. She got really upset and I felt so guilty.'

'What did you argue about?' asked Victoria.

'Oh, all sorts of things,' said Fliss vaguely. 'The play, mostly. She said she wished I'd never signed up for it.'

'No!' Mari was horrified. 'Doesn't she know how good you are?'

'It's not about that,' said Fliss, patting blusher onto her cheeks. 'She thinks it's making me rude and moody. And anyway, she thinks I should be studying.'

'Studying what?' asked Mari. 'It's the holidays! You can study again when we go back to school next week.' She leaned forward. 'You're all uneven. You've got more blusher on one cheek than the other. Let me have a go.'

Fliss closed her eyes obediently as Mari vigorously brushed blusher over one cheek. 'It's only because she never went to university,' she said. 'She wants me to do really well at school so I can have the opportunities she didn't.'

'But, Fliss,' said Mari, 'it's *your* life, not hers.'

'I know that,' said Fliss, 'but I don't want to let her down, you know?'

Victoria nodded. 'I understand. And she did bring you up on her own. You feel like you owe her.'

'That's exactly it.'

Mari sat down on a stool, a worried expression on her face. 'But, Fliss, you can't go through your life trying to please everyone else. You can't make decisions just to make your mum happy. What about what *you* want?'

'But what if she's right?' said Fliss, trying to see herself in a small hand mirror. 'What if it would be better for me to do something normal with my life? There's no money in acting, everyone says so. Am I just wasting my life if I put all my efforts into it?'

She frowned. 'Mari, I look like I've dunked my face in strawberry ice cream! You've put far too much on!'

Victoria handed over a packet of baby wipes. 'Take it all off and start again.'

'You're not wasting your life,' said Mari, determined to continue the topic. 'You're good, you're really good. Even Candy says so.'

'But she's just one person,' said Fliss, scrubbing her face. 'And Mum said she's only a college teacher, so how would she know?'

'That is such a catty thing to say!' cried Mari. 'Surely if you're good, you're good. Candy's taught loads of people. *And* she did stuff for the BBC. She'd know talent when it came along. Your mum doesn't have a clue.'

Fliss flushed. 'She's only doing what she thinks is best for me.'

'Mari, I think you're being a bit harsh,' said Victoria. 'It's natural that Fliss's mum wants her to have a good career. And you *know* acting isn't very secure.'

Mari looked mulish. 'It is if you're good enough.'

'Well, let's not talk about it now,' said Fliss, sweeping the blusher brush across her face. 'Is that OK?'

'You look lovely,' said Victoria.

Samantha strode into the tent. 'Hello?' she shouted. 'Everyone listen!' The chatter died down a bit. Samantha frowned and tapped her foot. 'I'm waiting.'

Mari glanced at Fliss and rolled her eyes. 'Why does she have to make herself sound so important all the time?' she muttered.

'Mari, if you have something to say, maybe you'd like to share it with all of us?' said Samantha in a sneery voice.

Victoria grabbed Mari's arm before she could speak. 'No, no, she's finished. Honestly.'

'Fine,' said Samantha. 'This is a call for beginners. We're about to start.'

'That's me,' said Victoria, smoothing her hair back. 'See you guys in a bit.'

'Break a leg,' Fliss called after her.

Samantha turned to look at them. Her gaze slid over Mari and came to rest on Fliss. There was something odd in her expression. 'Yeah,' she said. 'You too, Fliss. Break a leg.' Then she turned and went out of the tent.

Mari stared after her. 'What was that about?'

'No idea,' Fliss said slowly. 'Weird, though.'

Mari shrugged. 'She's probably realized that after this weekend she's got no reason to hate you any more. Dress rehearsal tomorrow, then performance on Saturday. Then it's all over.'

'I wish we were doing more performances,' said Fliss, smoothing out the creases in her dress. 'All this work for just one show! It seems so unfair.'

'Better make it count then,' said Mari.

'Yeah . . .' Fliss's thoughts turned to Tom. If she were honest, her thoughts had almost all been about Tom since the last rehearsal. Even though she kept telling herself it was all useless, still she couldn't help dreaming . . . And Mari's words had just made everything so much more intense. After this weekend, it was all over. No more play, no more Tom – no more *kissing* Tom, that was more to the point. Back to seeing him on the bus on the way to school – back to real life.

Victoria came back into the tent, scowling. 'I know Candy said everything had been dried off, but the grass is still wet. Nearly sprained my ankle coming off the stage. Be careful of your shoes.'

'Hope you'll be OK on that balcony, Fliss,' said Mari.

Victoria shook her head. 'She'll be fine. Candy said she and Samantha personally dried every part of the set an hour ago.'

Fliss stood up. 'Nearly us, Mari. I want to make sure we don't miss our cue.'

Fliss had only seen Tom from a distance since the storm, so when it was time for the party scene, she found her heart gave an enormous thump. There he was – looking tall and serious and good-looking as ever. Those eyes . . .

But something was different. Tom was saying his lines in the same way as usual, but although it looked like he was gazing into her eyes, he wasn't. Fliss frowned under her party mask. Why was he looking at the top of her head? Or at her ear? It was almost as though . . . almost as though he couldn't bear to look at her . . .

The kiss, when it came, was cold. Fliss felt nothing; it was as though Tom had no feelings at all. She wanted to cry. It seemed that their encounter in the storm had made things worse than ever. Now he hated her so much he couldn't even look at her!

By the time Fliss prepared to climb the balcony ladder, she was almost ready to give up. Maybe her mum was right after all. Maybe she *should* stop doing the play. But in her heart, Fliss knew she couldn't do that. It would be letting everyone down. And after all, it was only for another couple of days. The dress rehearsal tomorrow, and then the Saturday performance.

She took a deep breath and reached out for the

ladder. As Candy had promised, it was perfectly dry. It was nearly time. She gripped the sides of the ladder as she had been shown, put her foot on the first rung, and started to climb. She was so busy concentrating on holding up her skirt that when her foot slipped on the top rung, it took a split second to realize something was wrong. In panic, she reached out to the back of the balcony to steady herself, but her second foot, now also on the top rung, slipped too and Fliss completely lost her grip.

Frantic to catch hold of something – anything, Fliss toppled backwards . . .

Chapter 13

a dreadful shock

As Fliss lay on the grass and stared at the sky, she wondered why it was she hadn't fainted. People always fainted in books after falling off things. It was far more romantic. And it also meant you didn't have to be aware of people milling round you, treading on your hair by accident and saying things like, 'Oh my gosh, are you OK?' when it was plainly obvious she wasn't OK at all.

Mari was first by her side. 'Fliss, oh God! Don't move. Can you hear me? Blink if you can hear me.'

'I can hear you,' said Fliss, though the effort of speaking sent a shot of pain through her head. 'Ow.' She lifted an arm to her head, but that hurt too. 'Ow again.'

'You might have broken something,' said Mari, sounding panicked. 'We should lift your legs above your head.'

'What?'

'To get more blood to your brain. I'm sure that's right.'

Thankfully at this moment Candy arrived, flanked by Samantha and Tom. 'Fliss! You fell off the ladder? My goodness, I never imagined . . . ! Samantha dried that ladder only this lunch time!'

'That's right,' said Samantha, though Fliss noticed through her muggy state that Samantha was staring at her with a very strange intensity.

'She's hurt her head,' said Mari, 'and her arm, I think.'

'My wrist . . .' said Fliss faintly. Her head was starting to throb badly, and the trees above were getting fuzzy.

'We have to get her to Accident and Emergency,' said Candy practically. 'I'll call an ambulance.'

'An ambulance?' Tom was standing by Fliss now, looking down. He was pale. 'Is she – are you hurt badly?'

Fliss blinked, but the pain in her head was getting worse. 'I'm OK,' she said, and tried to sit up. But a wave of dizziness overcame her and she fell backwards. Tom caught her, his hands gentle under her head.

'Don't try to move. Really. Stay still.'

Candy was on the phone. Her voice was calm and efficient. 'Yes, she fell off a ladder. We're in the town park. There's a tarmac path through, past the lake. Yes. All right. No, we haven't moved her. OK.' She hung up. 'They'll be here in a few minutes.' She suddenly became aware of how many people were crowding round. 'Can everyone just keep back, please? In fact, can you all just go back to the tents and wait. Samantha . . .'

Samantha immediately took control. 'Right, you've seen enough. She's going to be fine. Come on, back this way.'

'I'm not going anywhere,' said Mari firmly.

'Me neither,' said Victoria, who looked like she was about to cry. 'She's my best friend.'

'Then you two can get her some blankets,' said Candy. 'We need to keep her warm, and this grass is wet. We don't want her catching a chill on top of everything else.'

Mari looked uncertain. 'I'll stay with her,' said Tom. Mari nodded, and she and Victoria went off.

'You don't have to stay, Tom,' said Candy. 'I've got her.'

'I want to.'

Fliss looked up, but it was becoming harder and harder to keep her eyes open. It was like someone had her head in a vice and was slowly squeezing it. 'Tom?' she whispered.

His voice came immediately, reassuring and calm. 'It's OK, Fliss. I'm here.'

'I'm sorry,' Fliss whispered.

He looked puzzled. 'What for?'

'For when I said . . .' Fliss's eyebrows creased in pain.

'Stop talking, Fliss,' said Candy firmly. 'Keep your eyes closed. Just rest. The ambulance will be here any minute. And I'll call your mum now, let her know what's happened.'

From a long way away, Fliss heard Samantha call something. The warm pressure on her hands suddenly lifted, and she knew Tom had gone. Something soft was placed over her, and she heard Mari say, 'Has she passed out?' and Candy reply, 'No, she's resting.' And then it was too hard to think, so she let her brain drift to a place where her head and her wrist didn't hurt so much.

♥

'I put two spoonfuls of sugar in it,' said Jeanette, placing a cup of tea by Fliss's bed. 'Sugar is good for shock.' She sat down gently and stroked Fliss's unbandaged right hand. The left one was heavily strapped. 'My poor little girl,' she said quietly, and Fliss felt her eyes fill with tears.

They had spent several hours in hospital as Fliss was thoroughly checked over. In the end, there was no lasting damage, although her wrist was badly sprained. The doctor said she had just bumped her head and after a day or two she would feel much better. 'Lots of rest,' he'd said.

'Of course, Doctor,' Jeanette had said fervently. 'I won't let her out of bed.'

He laughed. 'No need to be that drastic. But plenty of rest to get over the shock.'

Fliss didn't think her mother had even listened to the doctor's reply. Certainly as soon as they'd got home, Jeanette had ushered her upstairs and into bed. It was late now – just past midnight – and Jeanette looked pale with worry. Still she wouldn't leave Fliss's side. 'Would you like another pillow? I could read to you. I used to read to you when you were little. Would you like that or would it hurt your head?'

Fliss didn't know what to say. Everything ached and she felt very tired. 'I just want to sleep,' she whispered.

Jeanette's face softened. 'Of course, sweetheart.

At least they said you didn't have concussion. You sleep all you like. You've had a dreadful shock. We both have. Falling off a ladder! That Candy woman should never have allowed it to happen.' She looked down at her daughter again, and sighed. 'Thank goodness it wasn't any worse. You stay here now and rest. You need it.' She kissed Fliss very lightly on the forehead and went out, pulling the door to behind her.

Fliss lay on her back and stared at the ceiling. Her head throbbed, but it was the realization that she would not be able to act in the play that hurt the most. All that rehearsal! All that time with Tom! All wasted!

Her mind went back to the accident again and again. How could she have slipped? The rungs were dry, she knew they were. She must have just lost her footing. Not concentrating properly. Fliss frowned. It wasn't right. She had been up and down that ladder lots of times before. And why was it only on the top rung that she had slipped?

There was something . . . something wrong . . . something that was there that shouldn't have been there. But what was it?

Fliss's eyes opened wide as she replayed the

moment in her mind. The top rung was slippery. Not the other rungs . . . just the top one . . . but then that meant . . .

She breathed out as the realization came sharp and clear. Surely not! But if that was the case, then . . . Her eyes automatically went to the carpet by the door, where her shoes were lying neatly. She had to know!

Fliss got painfully out of bed and reached for the shoes. She turned them over with her good hand. Her breath caught in her throat. She was right! But then . . . who . . . ?

Fliss lay awake in bed for some time, puzzling it out, before sleep overcame her and she sank back into darkness.

♥

'That Candy is downstairs,' said Jeanette the next morning. 'I've told her you're not well enough to see anyone.'

Fliss pulled herself up on her pillows. 'Mum! I'm fine! My head hurts much less now.' Which was true, though it did still ache a bit, and she felt very tired. 'Please let her come up.'

Jeanette looked undecided. 'Well, she's not to stay

long. I've told her you can't do the play. Today or
tomorrow. She knows that already.'

Candy came in with a bunch of roses. 'I brought
these for you.' She smiled. 'You look a lot better than
you did yesterday.'

'Thanks. They're lovely.'

Candy sat down on a chair. 'Listen, Fliss, I just
came to tell you not to worry about anything. These
things happen. It's unfortunate but life goes on. It's
much more important that you stay here and rest.'
She smiled again. 'I am so relieved you're not badly
hurt. I had someone check out the ladder after you'd
gone off in the ambulance.'

'And?' Fliss's voice sharpened.

Candy shook her head. 'I can't see how you fell off.
It wasn't rickety or anything, and it was quite dry. You
must just have missed your footing or something.'

Fliss hesitated a moment. 'I expect you're right,' she
said eventually.

'Anyway,' said Candy, 'Samantha has stepped into
the breach. I didn't realize she knew all your lines.
Such luck, her having been in all the rehearsals so she
knows the blocking and everything.'

Fliss managed a half-smile. 'Such luck,' she
echoed.

'Of course,' said Candy, with a small sigh, 'she's

not you.' She bit her lip. 'I am *very* sorry you won't be able to perform, Fliss. Even if you'd missed the dress rehearsal and come in for the final show, I feel confident you'd be able to give a wonderful performance. And I've got a friend coming – I've been telling him all about you. He's in the business, you see – well, never mind now. Your mum says you've got to have complete rest for a week. Such bad luck.' She sighed again and got up. 'You just look after yourself and, like I said, don't worry about anything. The show must go on!' She smiled gently. 'And get yourself better in time for the next production, OK?'

Fliss did her best to smile back. 'OK,' she said.

As soon as Candy had gone, Fliss texted Mari and Victoria. She knew Jeanette wouldn't approve, but she had to see her friends as soon as possible. There was something vitally important she had to tell them!

♥

'I'm sorry,' Jeanette said at the door. 'She's supposed to have complete rest.'

'But she asked us to come,' said Mari. She held up her phone. 'She sent us a text.'

Jeanette frowned. 'She shouldn't have. I'll go and have a word.'

Fliss was sitting up in bed, straining to hear the conversation downstairs. Jeanette pushed open the door, looking annoyed. 'Mari and Victoria are here. Did you text them?'

'Mum,' said Fliss, 'there's something I have to tell them. Something really important.'

'I don't care what it is,' said Jeanette. 'You're not well. You shouldn't be seeing anyone.'

'Please, Mum,' said Fliss. 'I wouldn't ask normally. You know I wouldn't.'

Jeanette sighed. 'What is it? This really important thing?'

'I can't tell you,' admitted Fliss. 'But I will. If it turns out to be true. Honestly.'

'Is it something to do with the play?' asked Jeanette suspiciously.

'Sort of,' said Fliss. 'But please don't worry. I'm not trying to get back into it.'

Jeanette hesitated.

'Please,' said Fliss. 'This is really important to me. Please.'

Jeanette shook her head. 'They mustn't stay long. Only a few minutes.'

'All right,' said Fliss.

Mari and Victoria came creeping into the room as though they were expecting Fliss to shatter into a thousand pieces at their step. 'Oh,' said Victoria in surprise. 'You haven't even got a bandage on your head.'

'Didn't need one,' said Fliss. 'I didn't cut my head.'

'How's your wrist though?' asked Mari, looking at the heavy strapping.

'Sore,' said Fliss, 'but that's not why I called you guys.' She glanced towards the door. 'We might not have much time, but I had to see you.'

Mari settled herself on the end of the bed, a look of intense curiosity on her face. 'What's going on?'

'It's to do with my accident,' said Fliss.

'Yes?'

'Well, the thing is . . .' Fliss paused, then the words came out with a rush. 'The thing is it may not have been an accident at all.'

Mari and Victoria both jolted backwards in shock. 'What!' exclaimed Victoria. 'What do you mean?'

'That top rung,' said Fliss earnestly. 'You know, the one where I slipped.'

Mari nodded. 'Candy said you must have mistimed it.'

Fliss shook her head. 'I didn't. I know I didn't. There was something on that top rung.'

Victoria looked confused. 'What sort of something?'

'Oil,' said Fliss. 'There was oil on the top rung.'

There was a sudden silence.

'Oil?' said Victoria slowly. 'But why would there be oil . . .'

Mari let out her breath with a whoosh. 'Oh my. You're not saying . . . you *are* saying . . .'

'It was slippery,' said Fliss. 'Not dry, like the other rungs. Just that one. There was no grip at all.'

'But this is serious,' said Mari.

'I know.'

Victoria was looking bewildered. 'I don't understand. Why would there be oil on the ladder?'

'There wouldn't,' said Mari, 'unless someone put it there.'

'But why would someone put oil on it?' asked Victoria.

Mari made a noise of frustration. 'You are so slow, Vic! Think about it! Fliss is the only one to go up that ladder, right? And who wanted Fliss's part right from the start? Who wanted to play Juliet more than anything? Who would do anything to put Fliss out of the way?'

Victoria's face paled under her natural coffee-colour. 'You can't mean Samantha?'

'Who else?'

'But she wouldn't!' said Victoria. 'I mean – no one would do that! Fliss might have been killed!'

'Well, I don't know about that,' said Fliss uncomfortably. 'It was only about eight feet up, wasn't it?'

'That's high enough to break your neck,' said Mari. 'People do that when they fall off horses. They're about the same height.'

Victoria shook her head and held up her hands. 'Whoa, whoa, guys. This is a serious accusation. Besides, how do we know for a fact that she did it?'

Mari looked at Fliss.

'We don't,' said Fliss slowly. 'I can't prove it was her. But I know what happened. Candy told me this morning that she'd checked the ladder after I'd gone off to hospital.'

'And?'

Fliss shrugged. 'She found nothing.'

'But by then, Samantha would have been able to clean off the oil,' said Mari. 'There was so much confusion after you fell.'

'She took everyone back to the tents,' objected Victoria. 'She wouldn't have had time.'

'Did you see her while Fliss was being lifted into the ambulance though?' asked Mari. 'I mean, could you actually *swear* she wasn't by the ladder for any of that time?'

'No-o,' said Victoria reluctantly.

'It would only have taken a few seconds,' said Mari. 'With a cloth. She could have been up and down the ladder before anyone noticed she'd gone.'

'Then when Candy checked the ladder herself,' said Fliss, 'it would have been perfectly dry again.'

Mari stared at Fliss. 'What are you going to do?'

'What can I do?' asked Fliss. 'I can't prove it was her.'

'But now she's playing your part!' said Mari. She smacked a fist into her other hand. 'Oh, it makes me so mad! We have to do something!'

Victoria held up her hands. 'Look, hang on a minute, guys. I believe you, Fliss, I really do. But we can't even prove there was oil on the ladder. Let alone prove it was Samantha who put it there.'

'I *can* prove that, actually,' said Fliss. She reached behind her bed and brought out the ballet pumps she had been wearing the afternoon before. 'My shoes.'

Victoria looked blank. 'What about them?'

'Of course!' Mari grabbed one of them and turned it over. 'Look! Oil marks on the bottom!'

There was a stunned silence.

'My God,' said Victoria in a hushed voice. 'Someone really did do it deliberately.'

'But this proves it!' said Mari. 'All we have to do is take the shoes to Candy and tell her what happened!'

Fliss shook her head. 'I thought of that. How can we prove it was Samantha who did it? There's nothing to link her with anything. It's not enough.'

Mari's forehead creased in frustration. 'But you can't let her get away with it.'

'I don't see . . .' said Victoria slowly. 'I mean, we have no proof. Fliss is right.'

Mari looked obstinate. 'We'll just have to come up with a way to prove it.'

There were footsteps on the stairs. Fliss shot a warning glance at her two friends as Jeanette came into the room, looking flustered. 'I quite lost track of the time,' she said. 'I was on the phone to Vivienne, and I didn't realize you two were still up here.' She gestured towards Mari and Victoria. 'Come on. You've been here long enough. Fliss needs to rest. She's still weak from the accident.'

'I was thinking she was looking a bit better,

actually,' said Mari, glancing towards her friend.

Jeanette frowned at Mari's tone of voice, but glancing at Fliss, she had to admit that her daughter had more colour in her cheeks than she'd had since yesterday. 'Well, even so, time's up,' she said decisively.

'But we haven't finished discussing the thing we were discussing,' said Fliss.

'Bad luck,' said Jeanette. 'Come on. Out.'

Mari stood up. 'We'll think about it,' she told Fliss meaningfully. 'You got your phone with you?'

'She's not leaving this house,' said Jeanette suspiciously. 'I know it's the dress rehearsal this afternoon. She's not going.'

'We know, Ms Richards,' said Victoria. 'Don't worry. We're not trying to persuade Fliss to act in the dress rehearsal.'

'Or the performance,' said Jeanette. 'She's out of the play completely, you understand?'

Mari and Victoria nodded. 'See you then, Fliss,' said Mari. She leaned forward to hug her friend and whispered in her ear, 'I'm not giving up. Keep your phone on.'

Fliss nodded. As she waved her friends out of the room, she felt all mixed up. Mari was right, she couldn't let Samantha get away with it. But Victoria was right too – they had no proof!

Samantha wasn't stupid. How could they ever prove it was her?

Fliss lay back on her pillows, her head spinning. There *must* be a way, there *must* . . .

Chapter 14

I can't do that!

Mari rang Fliss at lunchtime, two hours before the dress rehearsal was due to start. 'We haven't come up with anything,' she said in a depressed tone.

Fliss felt a wave of disappointment. 'Neither have I,' she admitted.

'I wanted to plant some oil in her bag,' said Mari, 'but Victoria went ballistic. Said it was completely immoral or something.'

'You could get in trouble for doing something like that,' said Fliss.

'I don't care,' said Mari. 'You should see her, Fliss. We're at the park. She's trying on your costumes right now, and she's being so smug about the whole thing. Laughing about how short your skirts look on her and how she's going to be a much sexier Juliet. Keeps flicking her hair around and asking everyone if she should wear it up or down. And how sorry she is about your accident but she's sure you'll be OK because, after all, skulls are very thick.' She made a noise of disgust. 'She makes me sick. But I don't want you to get in trouble. We need to catch her out fair and square.' She sighed. 'But I can't think of anything. Except . . .'

'What?'

Mari paused. 'You won't like it.'

'Just tell me.'

'Well,' said Mari, 'I think maybe if Samantha is confronted with the evidence – you know, your shoes and everything – I think we might stand a chance that she'd give herself away.'

Fliss thought for a moment. 'That could work. Do you want to come get my shoes?'

'No.' Mari hesitated again. 'That's the thing. I think *you* have to do it.'

'What do you mean?'

'You have to confront her, Fliss. You have to be the one to face her. It won't have the same effect if we do it.'

Fliss nearly dropped the phone. 'Are you *crazy*? I can't do that!'

'You have to,' said Mari. 'You have to be the one to say what really happened.'

'You would do it so much better than me,' said Fliss, feeling as though she might faint from fright. 'You're good at standing up to people. All that confidence. You know it's not my thing.'

'Look here, Fliss.' Mari's voice suddenly sharpened. 'Do you want justice done or not?'

Fliss squirmed. 'Well . . .'

'Because if you don't,' said Mari, 'then you might just as well lie around in bed and mope for the next week. Do you really want Samantha to get away with it? Seriously? Do you really want her to play Juliet tomorrow?'

'My mum said . . .'

'Never mind your mum. You're fine, you know you are. Even the doctor said you'd be OK within forty-eight hours, didn't he? And Candy said you'd be perfectly capable of doing the performance even if you'd missed the dress rehearsal.'

'Yes, but . . .'

'Does your head still hurt?'

'No.'

'And you can easily play Juliet with your wrist strapped up.'

'How would I get onto the balcony?' objected Fliss.

Mari tutted in frustration. 'Someone will help you. I'll get Sean to give you a leg up.'

'Sean? Do you mean you . . .'

'Yes, yes,' said Mari impatiently. 'I asked him if he fancied me and he said yes. We're going out, sort of. Next week maybe.'

'But that's amazing!'

'We'll see. But that's not what we're discussing here.' Mari took a deep breath. Then she said, 'Fliss, we know you. You don't like to stand up to people. But this is about your dream. You love playing Juliet. You're crazy about Tom. This is your big chance. Are you really going to let a sneaky, weaselly, rat-faced creep take it all away from you?'

Fliss was silent. Could she really do it? It would be the scariest thing she had ever done. Far scarier than being on stage. She'd have to confront Samantha in front of everyone. Every part of her body screamed in terror at the thought.

But on the other hand, if she did nothing, then Samantha had won, hadn't she? If it really was her who spread oil on the ladder – if Fliss said nothing then Samantha would get away with it. And maybe she'd think she could do things like that to other people too. Not to mention the fact that Samantha would be playing Juliet, the part Fliss had wanted to play for so long. She wouldn't get another chance like this. Maybe it would work, maybe it wouldn't. But if she never tried, she'd always wonder.

'Fliss?' Mari's voice came down the phone. 'You still there?'

Fliss took a deep breath and let it out very slowly. She held the phone to her ear. 'All right. I'll do it.'

Mari let out a whoop. 'She'll do it!' Fliss heard her say to Victoria. 'Right,' Mari said, becoming practical. 'I think you should sneak in so that no one knows you're there. That way, when you accuse Samantha, she'll be even more shocked . . .'

♥

The next couple of hours felt like days to Fliss. Jeanette bustled in and out with cups of tea and tiny sandwiches, 'Just in case you feel tempted.' Fliss was ravenous and asked for more. Jeanette was surprised. 'I thought you might have lost your appetite.'

'I'm not *ill*, Mum.'

Jeanette felt her forehead. 'You're a bit hot.'

'No, I'm not. You're imagining things.'

Jeanette looked hurt. 'I just want to make sure you're all right.'

'I know, Mum. And I do appreciate it, really.' Fliss patted the bed beside her. 'Stop rushing around all the

time. I feel bad enough you've had to take the day off
work. I'm fine, honestly.'

'Your head doesn't hurt?'

'No.'

'What about your wrist?'

'That is sore,' admitted Fliss, 'but only if I lift it
above my head. It doesn't really hurt if I don't move
it about.'

Jeanette sank onto the bed with a sigh. 'You hear
such terrible things about people who've banged
their heads. Think they're OK and then two hours
later they fall down dead.'

'It's been way over two hours,' said Fliss gently.
'And the doctor did check me over at the hospital. He
wouldn't have sent me home if he thought there was
anything to worry about.'

'I know.' Jeanette rubbed her eye. 'I can't help it,
that's all. I don't want to . . . lose you.'

Fliss felt a wave of sympathy for her mother. 'Oh
Mum, you're not going to lose me.'

'Aren't I?' Jeanette looked at her. 'You're growing up
so fast,' she said sadly. 'You don't tell me everything
any more.'

'What do you mean? Of course I do!'

'No, you have secrets you only tell your friends,'
said Jeanette. 'Like this morning. What could

you tell Mari and Victoria that you couldn't tell me?'

Fliss reached forward to put her good arm around her mum. 'I will tell you, honestly,' she said. 'Later today. It's something I have to face up to. I've been a scaredy-cat for too long.'

Jeanette stroked her hair. 'That's probably my fault, isn't it?' she said with a sigh. 'I protect you too much, I know I do.'

'You're my mum, you're supposed to look after me.'

'I get it all wrong,' said Jeanette, shaking her head. 'I only want what's best for you, but it always seems to come out wrong.'

Fliss pulled back to look into her mum's eyes. 'You don't get it wrong,' she said gently. 'Maybe some-times I'm just ungrateful. I know you're only trying to make sure I have a good future. I should listen to you more.'

'But I don't listen to *you* enough, do I?' asked Jeanette. 'I worry so much about you making the right decisions, I don't ask you what you want.' She sighed again. 'Being a mother is the hardest thing I've ever done.'

Fliss gave her another hug. 'You do it really well. Honest.'

Jeanette squeezed her back. 'You are the best daughter in the world. And I will try to listen more to what you want. I know being in this play meant a lot to you. I've booked my ticket, you know. Maybe we can both go and watch it tomorrow, eh? It won't be sold out, will it?'

Fliss smiled. 'That sounds good.'

Jeanette touched her gently on the nose. 'I love you, Felicity.'

Fliss felt her eyes fill with tears. 'I love you too. And you're a great mum. I know you only want me to be happy.'

Jeanette hugged her again and Fliss hugged her back, but inside she felt like a traitor. Here she was, promising to be a better daughter, when she knew that within an hour she would be slipping out of the house against her mum's wishes. Jeanette had just told her she was the best daughter in the world – and she was about to betray that trust. But if she didn't, she would lose the chance to fight for her dreams.

Fliss buried her face in her mother's shoulder and wished there were another way.

♥

'She's still not here,' Victoria whispered to Mari, as they both peered anxiously through a crack in the set. 'We're nearly at the end.'

'Maybe she's hiding round the corner until the right moment,' said Mari.

'Maybe she's not coming,' said Victoria.

Mari turned to face her friend. 'She has to come!' she hissed. 'She agreed!'

'But this is Fliss we're talking about,' argued Victoria. 'You know she's terrified of confrontation . . .'

'Sssh!' said several people.

Mari took Victoria's hand and they headed back along the path towards the tent. When they could be sure they were out of earshot, they stopped and stared at each other. 'She has to come,' said Mari again, but her voice was uncertain.

Victoria sighed. 'I miss her. It's not the same without her.'

'You're so right,' said Mari, glancing back the way they had come. 'Samantha is murdering the lines.'

'She just sounds so *harsh*,' said Victoria.

'Nasal,' Mari said, pursing her lips. 'Sounds like she's talking through her nose. And she's not even getting the words right.'

Victoria frowned in puzzlement. 'Is that what it is? I thought the words sounded a bit different but I assumed it was because it was a different person saying them.'

Mari shook her head. 'She's making half of them up. They're nearly right, but little words here and there are wrong.'

'I suppose Candy is just grateful that there's someone who knows any of the lines at all,' mused Victoria.

'It would have been better if they'd got someone in to read the lines from the book than have Samantha do it,' said Mari.

'Oh, come on,' said Victoria. 'She's not that bad. Her voice is a bit annoying, and she's making some little mistakes, but she's doing OK. I mean, if we hadn't been used to Fliss doing it, we might even have thought Samantha was quite good.'

'I wouldn't,' said Mari. 'She stomps around as though she owns the stage. She doesn't wait for you to finish your lines – she interrupted me twice in one of our scenes. And did you see the way she flirted with Tom in the balcony scene? Juliet wouldn't do that. Samantha was outrageous!'

'Well, unless Fliss turns up, Samantha will be doing it for real tomorrow,' said Victoria.

'I don't think Tom would be impressed,' said Mari, her mouth twitching into a reluctant smile. 'Did you see him when they were meant to be kissing? He could hardly bear to touch her. I reckon that relationship isn't going to last.'

'It's too late for Fliss though, isn't it?' said Victoria sadly. 'She's given up on him.'

'Don't you believe it,' Mari began, but she stopped as she saw a familiar tall figure with red hair coming towards them. 'Sean,' she said coolly. 'You OK?'

'Yeah,' said Sean. 'Just came to say we're nearly at the last speech. Candy wants everyone on stage to practise the bow.'

'Oh, cheers,' said Mari.

Sean hesitated, then turned to go.

'Oh, by the way,' Mari suddenly said.

Sean turned back, his face lit up with expectation. 'Yes?'

'Your left sleeve is torn,' Mari pointed out.

'What?' Sean twisted to see. He swore. 'Mrs Carstairs is gonna kill me!'

'You are naughty,' said Victoria to Mari as they watched Sean head off again. 'He thought you were going to say something sweet.'

'Treat 'em mean, keep 'em keen,' said Mari. 'Don't

want him to think I'm too easy to please, do I? He won't make the effort.'

Victoria shook her head in amusement. 'Where do you get these ideas?'

'Oh, come on,' said Mari. 'Everyone knows you've got to play hard to get. At least a little bit. Boys like the thrill of the chase.'

Victoria let out a snort. 'You read too many magazines.'

They headed back to the stage. The Prince was just declaiming the last lines of the play: 'For never was a story of more woe than this of Juliet and her Romeo.'

'Good,' came Candy's voice from the audience. 'Can I have everyone on stage please?'

Mari and Victoria clambered up behind the other cast members, and Candy began sorting them out into groups. 'You guys come on first – from stage right. Stage *right*, Simone, that's the *other* side. And this group, you come on next. From stage left this time. First group, you move to the back of the stage so the next lot can have a bow . . .'

♥

From the shadow of a tree, Fliss watched the company shuffle around the stage, and felt as though her knees might give way. Sneaking out of the house had been easier than expected, since Jeanette had had to go to the shops for more bread and milk. Fliss had felt terrible about it. She'd left a note, telling Jeanette she had to do something important, but she knew her mother would be angry with her, especially after the conversation they'd just had. And now that she was here, clutching her shoes in her hand, a large part of her wished she'd just stayed at home. How could she possibly face Samantha in front of everyone? More than ever Fliss wished she'd had the courage to tell Candy what she suspected. But then, would Candy have believed her?

The curtain call practice was coming to an end, and Samantha and Tom were taking their bows. Samantha wore such a smug expression on her face that Fliss felt the anger rise inside her. How dare Samantha look so self-satisfied? She might at least have the decency to look modest; to give off the air of, 'well, I only got the part by a piece of luck.' Instead she was stalking from one side of the stage to the other, giving several bows and acting as though she were the best in the play. By contrast,

Tom looked somehow smaller as he watched her in bewilderment.

'I think that will do, Samantha,' said Candy drily. 'Four bows is quite enough for anyone.'

Samantha let out a silly laugh. 'But I am the leading lady. Surely I get a couple more?'

Before she knew what she was doing, Fliss had moved out of the shadows and towards the stage. A small gasp went up from the cast members who caught sight of her. 'Fliss!'

Mari and Victoria, standing towards the back, looked up and saw her too. 'Fliss!' yelled Mari. 'I knew you'd come!'

But Fliss only had eyes for Samantha, who had gone quite white. 'Hello, Samantha,' she said.

'Fliss,' said Candy, 'you shouldn't be here. You should be resting.'

'Well,' said Fliss, her eyes still firmly fixed on Samantha, 'I would be, Candy, but there was something I had to come to tell you.'

Candy looked puzzled. 'What, here? Now?'

Fliss nodded. If she kept her feet planted firmly on the ground, somehow she didn't feel so nervous. 'You see, Candy, when I fell off the balcony ladder – well, it wasn't exactly an accident.'

There was a sudden murmur from the cast on stage.

Many of them were staring at Fliss in astonishment. Victoria reached for Mari's hand and gripped it tight. 'Go on, girl,' muttered Mari.

'Not an accident?' Candy's jaw dropped. 'What are you talking about?'

'When I was lying in bed late last night,' said Fliss, her voice calm and steady, 'I kept going over and over it in my head. And I realized something.'

The whispers on stage suddenly fell silent. 'Fliss, I don't think this is quite the time or the place . . .' Candy said, but Fliss held up a hand.

'Please,' she said. 'I have to do this here and now. Because what I realized was . . . *oil*.'

Samantha suddenly stumbled, and Fliss knew from the look on her face that she had been right to suspect her. 'Ouch!' cried Samantha. 'I've twisted my ankle.' But nobody took any notice.

'Oil?' said Candy, confused. 'Oil where?'

'On the top rung of the ladder,' said Fliss. 'Not on any of the other rungs. Just the top one. Which is why my feet slipped.'

Candy was shaking her head. 'There wasn't any oil, Fliss. I checked the ladder after you'd gone. Honestly. It was dry as a bone.'

Fliss nodded. 'It was dry *then*. That's because someone had had time to dry it with a cloth.'

Candy went very still. 'Fliss,' she said quietly, 'what exactly are you saying?'

Fliss looked Candy squarely in the eye. 'I'm saying someone deliberately tried to injure me.'

Chapter 15

what kind of sick person are you?

The buzz on stage erupted into full-blown uproar. Everyone was looking at each other, exclaiming, whispering behind their hands, glancing around. 'Quiet!' shouted Candy. 'Fliss, what you're saying is very serious. I really think we should talk about this in private. Not in front of everyone.' Candy started to walk towards Fliss. 'Come on, let's go and find somewhere we can talk.'

'No,' said Fliss firmly. Mari's hand tightened in Victoria's as the two of them hardly dared breathe. 'It has to be here and now.'

Candy's lips tightened. 'Fliss,' she said, 'I think you must be mistaken. There really wasn't any oil on that ladder, you know. I did check it. And Samantha and I dried the set ourselves. You must have imagined it.'

Fliss met her gaze levelly. Under her arm was the pair of shoes. She held them out. 'I didn't. Because there's oil on these. See for yourself.'

There was a dead silence. Only Samantha gave a small gasp, and Fliss felt a tiny flicker of satisfaction. Samantha hadn't thought of that, had she? She hadn't thought there would be any evidence!

Candy came towards Fliss and took the shoes from her. Slowly, she turned them over to examine the soles. On each shoe there was a skidmark. She ran her finger across one of them. 'It's oily,' she said in astonishment. Then she looked at Fliss.

'That could have got there from anything,' said Samantha suddenly. 'From – from walking along the road. Anything.'

Candy turned to look at her curiously. 'What do you mean? Since when does oil get onto shoes from the road?'

'I'm just *saying*,' said Samantha, but she was shifting from foot to foot uncomfortably. 'It mightn't have been the ladder.' Her expression changed. 'In fact,' she said, 'Fliss might even have put the oil on her shoes *herself*, to make us think there was oil on the ladder.'

Candy stared in disbelief. 'Are you suggesting Fliss would hurt herself on purpose? What on earth for?'

Samantha looked around nervously. The cast behind her were starting to mutter amongst themselves, and some of them were giving her very strange looks. 'To frame one of us, of course,' she said, and gave a laugh. Fliss's fingers tingled. Even to her ears the laugh sounded thin and false. 'To make herself look more important.'

'What are you talking about?' said Tom. 'Make herself look more important? *Fliss?*'

Samantha turned to him. 'Oh, you boys,' she said in a high voice. 'You never see what's going on right under your noses.' She looked around and laughed again. 'She's got you all fooled. Pretending to be so meek and shy. She just wants to be in the spotlight all the time.' Her gaze swung round to Fliss, and her nose wrinkled in disgust. 'Little princess, that's what she is.'

'I think that's enough, Samantha,' said Candy firmly.

'No,' said Fliss, 'let her speak.'

A ripple of surprise passed through the cast.

'Fliss,' said Candy, 'this isn't productive.'

'Yes it is,' said Fliss, though she was shaking. 'Because Samantha wanted to play Juliet herself.' She turned to face the tall blonde girl. 'Didn't you?'

Samantha stared at her. 'That's none of your business.'

'I think it is,' said Fliss. *You have to make her admit*

it, a little voice in her head was saying. *Keep going. The more she talks, the more likely she is to confess.* 'I think Samantha was jealous of me.'

Samantha laughed – far too loudly and far too long. 'Jealous?' she choked. 'Of *you*? Don't make me laugh! If anything, you were jealous of *me*, going out with Tom.'

Fliss willed herself not to look at Tom. 'What if I was?' she asked. 'You didn't need to worry. I was never a threat to you.'

'Oh, you say that,' said Samantha, and slowly the expression on her face was darkening, 'with your help-me-I'm-so-shy act. Had Tom wrapped around your little finger, didn't you? Couldn't stop talking about you! *Fliss said this, Fliss did that.* I was sick of hearing about you!'

Fliss nodded, though her heart was pounding. This was her opportunity! 'Is that why you put oil on the ladder?' she asked calmly.

'You deserved it!' said Samantha, and then clapped her hands to her mouth as she realized what she'd said.

The company gasped collectively. Mari and Victoria looked at each other in triumph. 'She did it!' whispered Victoria.

Other members of the cast started to gossip

excitedly to each other. 'I never would have believed she'd go that far!' Simone was saying.

Fliss felt her knees weaken in relief. She'd done it!

Candy held up her hands. 'Stop!' she shouted over the rising noise. 'Quiet, all of you! *Shut up!*'

The hubbub died down abruptly. 'Let me get this straight,' said Candy, her voice trembling with anger. 'Are you saying you spread oil on the ladder, Samantha? So that Fliss would fall off?'

'She didn't hurt herself that much,' said Samantha sulkily. 'I never meant her to *die* or anything.'

Tom stepped forward. His eyes were hard. 'You hurt Fliss on purpose?' he said. 'You injured Fliss so that you could play Juliet?'

She turned to him, and a pleading look came into her eyes. 'Tom, I only thought . . . it would be really good if we could play opposite each other . . . on stage . . .' Her voice trailed away as he glared at her.

'I can't believe I went out with you,' he said clearly. 'What kind of sick person are you?'

'But . . . Tom . . .' She reached out to him, but he turned his back.

'I don't ever want to see you again.'

Candy cleared her throat. 'This whole situation is getting out of hand,' she said firmly. 'The rehearsal is over. All of you, go back and get changed. I will see you an hour before curtain up tomorrow. Don't be late. Samantha, come here.'

Gradually, in small groups, the cast left the stage, muttering excitedly and casting glances back at Samantha and Fliss. 'Off you go too, Mari,' said Candy crisply, as Mari lingered at the back of the stage. Mari looked disgruntled, but she went with the others. Within moments, it was just the three of them. Fliss stood uncertainly on the grass. Her head was beginning to ache again, and she felt strangely light-headed. Had she really just done that? In front of everyone? She wasn't sure her legs would hold her up for much longer.

'Samantha,' said Candy, when she had come down from the stage, 'I think it goes without saying that you are officially fired from the production.'

Samantha nodded mutely. She seemed somehow smaller. All her brash confidence had gone. She was like a deflated balloon.

'Furthermore,' continued Candy, 'I think it only right that I inform your parents of what you did.'

'Oh, please don't!' Samantha exclaimed. 'My dad'll kill me.'

'Think yourself lucky that I'm not calling the police,' said Candy sharply.

Samantha's face went so white she looked like she might faint. 'What?' she whispered.

'What you did was a crime,' Candy told her. 'Intent to cause bodily harm, probably. Something like that. You deliberately set out to injure another person. No matter what you might think, you can't go around doing that kind of thing. It's a crime and punishable by law.'

'But you're not going to tell them?' Samantha whispered.

'No,' said Candy. 'That's up to Fliss.' They both turned to look at her. Samantha's eyes were wide with fright. Candy crossed her arms. 'She's the one who decides whether to report you or not.'

'Please,' said Samantha, so softly that Fliss barely heard her.

'It's up to you,' said Candy. 'Do you want to take this further?'

Fliss didn't know what to say. She had never imagined things could go that far. She opened her mouth but nothing came out.

'I'm so sorry,' said Samantha, seeing Fliss hesitate. 'I never thought . . . well, I guess I didn't think at all. I wanted to play Juliet so badly, and you seemed to have all the luck.' She swallowed. 'Even Tom . . . all he could ever talk about was you. When we went out, he never seemed to notice me. He was always thinking about you.' Her eyes filled with tears and her lower lip wobbled. 'I just wanted some of that limelight . . .'

A week ago – even an hour ago – Fliss would never have thought she could feel sorry for Samantha. But the girl was pathetic. She was broken and humiliated. 'I don't want to tell the police,' said Fliss. She suddenly felt very tired. 'I want to go home.'

Candy took hold of her arm. 'Of course. You shouldn't even be here. You should be resting.' She turned to Samantha. 'I think you should make yourself scarce.'

Samantha nodded. 'Thank you,' she said to Fliss in a shaky voice. 'Thank you. I'm so sorry.' Then she lowered her head and went.

'We'd better get you home,' said Candy. 'Does your mum know you're here?'

Fliss shook her head. 'I left a note, but I didn't say where I was going. She's probably guessed.'

'Sit down on the stage and I'll ring her,' said Candy. 'She'll be worried about you.'

'The play . . .' said Fliss, exhausted. 'Who's going to play Juliet?'

'Don't worry about that now,' said Candy.

'But Samantha . . .'

'We'll think of something. If the worst comes to the worst, we cancel.' Candy smiled at her. 'It's just a play.'

'I can do it,' said Fliss. 'I *want* to do it.'

'You're shattered,' said Candy. 'You need to go to bed.'

'But tomorrow,' said Fliss. 'I'll be better . . .'

Candy looked closely at her. She hesitated for a moment, and then said reluctantly, 'Maybe. We'll see.'

'My mum won't want me to do it. But I want to. Please.'

'I understand,' said Candy. 'Don't worry about a thing.' She looked anxiously at Fliss. 'Listen, here's a cushion from the Capulet party scene. Lie down for a minute. Close your eyes. I'll take care of everything.'

♥

Candy was as good as her word. Jeanette arrived, white and terrified, and Candy took her aside and had a long talk. Fliss lay back on the stage in the evening warmth and stared at the sky. Gradually all the other cast members went home, and still Candy and Jeanette were talking. Fliss watched the clouds change from white to pink to grey, and tried to think about what Samantha had said. Something about Tom . . . *He couldn't stop talking about you.* Why? It was all so confusing. Why would Tom go out with Samantha and then talk about Fliss all the time? Fliss let the thoughts drift in and out of her head like clouds on the breeze.

Eventually, Jeanette came over. 'Come on,' she said gently. 'Time to go home.'

Fliss allowed herself to be lifted up and supported back to the car. By the time she reached home she was already asleep. Jeanette looked across at her daughter. Fliss's head had fallen sideways, and her long dark eyelashes rested against her cheeks. Jeanette reached out a hand and stroked the side of her face. What an extraordinary thing for Fliss to have done today! Standing up in front of everyone and accusing that girl! Candy said she had been quite calm and strong. Jeanette could hardly believe it. Her little Felicity! Confronting someone! And, what's more, being proved right! Jeanette's face hardened as she thought about what that Samantha girl had done, spreading oil on the ladder. What a stupid, dangerous thing to do. Fliss could have been hurt far worse than she was. This must have been the thing she talked about with her friends. Jeanette felt sad that Fliss couldn't confide in her. But maybe, she thought, with a sudden realization, I wouldn't have taken her seriously. I was so concerned about her getting better, I wouldn't have listened properly.

Jeanette smiled at her daughter's sleeping face. 'I'll do better,' she promised in a whisper. 'I'll try to listen to you more. And as for tomorrow . . .' She sighed as she remembered what Candy had said about the play. 'We'll see how things look in the morning.'

Chapter 16

come with me

'I can't believe your mum let you come!' Mari squealed in excitement and threw her arms around Fliss.

'Ow! Mind my arm!' Fliss grinned as she patted her friend on the back. 'I'm still an invalid, you know.'

'Invalid, my foot,' said Mari, snorting. 'If you can stand up in front of everyone like you did yesterday, there's absolutely nothing wrong with you.'

Victoria smiled. 'Everyone's talking about it. You amazed us all.' She pulled a face. 'I didn't think you would do it. Not really.'

'I did,' said Mari confidently. 'I always knew you had it in you.'

'I am so lucky to have friends like you,' said Fliss.

Mari looked around in mock astonishment. 'Friends *like* us? You have other friends? Who are they? I'll stamp on their fingers!'

The other two laughed. 'You are so silly,' said Victoria. 'She meant us.'

'I know,' said Mari, sticking her tongue out. 'I was being daft on purpose.'

The three friends were sitting on the stage in the park, soaking up the late summer sun. 'Next week we'll be back at school,' said Victoria, with a sigh.

'It won't be so bad,' said Fliss. 'New year, new start, all that.'

'New *you*,' said Mari, digging her slyly in the ribs. 'New confidence.'

Victoria nodded. 'I shall call on you to fight all my battles for me in future.'

Fliss laughed. 'Don't you dare. Do you know how ill I felt after confronting Samantha?'

Victoria gave her a hug. 'Well, it was worth it, wasn't it?'

'Yes,' Fliss admitted. 'I never realized how good it could feel to stand up for yourself. I felt as if nothing could stop me.'

'You must have shocked your mum,' said Mari thoughtfully, 'for her to let you come today.'

'I think I did. I don't know what Candy told her, but Mum's being nicer than she's ever been before.' Fliss glanced over to the shade of a tree, where Jeanette sat reading a book. 'She wouldn't let me come out unsupervised though.'

'You're *here*, that's the main thing.' Victoria followed

Fliss's gaze. 'And when she sees you perform, she'll see how brilliant you are.'

Fliss pulled a face. 'I'm a bit nervous now though.'

'Don't be,' said Mari. 'Just think about how much you like acting.' She added, 'And how much you like Tom.'

Fliss blushed. She hadn't been able to stop thinking about what Samantha had said. 'He talked about you all the time,' she'd said. Was that really true? If it was . . .

'Candy's coming over,' said Victoria, standing up. 'She probably wants us to get ready.'

Candy called the group together on stage. 'You guys have worked so hard,' she said, her face alight with enthusiasm. 'You really deserve this. We'll do some warm-ups and then I want you to get into costume and get focused. I want you to put yesterday out of your minds. The audience will be arriving very soon. No messing about this afternoon, it's the real thing.' She turned to smile at Fliss. 'And welcome back, Fliss.'

The rest of the cast broke into spontaneous applause. Fliss blushed again, and found herself catching Tom's eye. He was clapping as hard as any of them, and his gaze was fixed firmly on Fliss. There was such warmth in his stare that she had to look away. Could it really be true? But there was no time to wonder about Tom now. Candy led them through a round of physical and vocal warm-ups, and then it was time to get into costume and put on makeup.

The girls' tent was strangely quiet as they got ready. 'I am so nervous,' said Victoria, rubbing her stomach. 'I think I might be sick. What if I forget my lines?'

'If you forget your lines,' Mari said, trying to put on mascara, 'then we can't even start the play. You've got the first one, remember!'

Victoria clapped her hand to her mouth. 'Oh no! What *is* the first line of the play?'

'Two households . . .' began Fliss.

'Oh yes, yes! Both alike in dignity!' Victoria flapped around like an oversized moth. 'Of course! How could I forget that?'

'I don't know,' said Mari, 'but if you don't sit still, you'll knock all my stuff onto the ground.'

Victoria clasped her hands behind her back. 'I'm so sorry. I just – Fliss, aren't you nervous?'

Fliss stared at herself in her little mirror. The reflection that stared back was of a serious-looking girl, with dark eyelashes and eyes, high cheekbones with a hint of pink, a small tilted nose and a rosebud mouth. It was the face she had always seen in the mirror. But today something felt different. 'No,' she said slowly. 'I don't think I am nervous.'

'After what you did yesterday, nothing should ever scare you again,' said Sarah, who was brushing her hair nearby. 'You were amazing!'

Fliss smiled. 'Thanks. But I was terrified.'

'Well, you did the right thing. I never liked Samantha, but wow! What she did to you! What a—'

'Let's not get into a slanging match,' said Fliss hurriedly. 'She wasn't very nice, but I think she was really insecure too. She did it because she was desperate.'

'You can't feel sorry for her,' said Sarah. 'Not after what she did to you.' She nodded towards Fliss's wrist, which was still heavily strapped. 'You could have broken that. Or your neck.'

'But I didn't,' said Fliss, thinking back to how Samantha had behaved once she knew she had been found out. She had been utterly humiliated, and she had begged Fliss not to report her to the police. 'It was all show. She was confident on the outside but not on the inside.'

'Not like you,' said Sarah with a grin, and she went back to brushing her hair.

'Hear that?' said Mari. 'Confident on the inside,

that's *you*. You don't need to play a character now to be confident.'

Candy came into the tent. 'Beginners please!'

Fliss looked at her friends. 'But it's time for all of us to play our parts,' she said. She gave a sudden smile. 'Thank you, both of you. I'd never have found the courage to do what I did if it hadn't been for you.'

Mari pretended to wipe her eyes. 'Aw, stop it, you'll make me cry.'

Fliss held out her arms. 'Group hug!' The three girls hugged each other. 'Now, off you go,' Fliss told Victoria, 'and it's "Two Households", all right?'

'Oh, good grief,' said Victoria. 'My hands are shaking.'

'Get on with it!' said Mari, pushing her out of the tent and laughing. When Victoria had gone, Mari turned to face Fliss. 'Now you,' she said. 'Just you make sure you go out there and blow them all away. Show your mum and everyone what you can do.'

♥

The applause was loudest for Fliss and Tom, and Fliss saw her mother sitting in the audience, clapping so hard her hands were a blur. She looked like she was trying not to cry. Fliss blew her a kiss, and the audience clapped even louder. Tom squeezed her hand, and she turned to look at him. It was as though for the first time that evening she was really seeing him properly – not through the eyes of Juliet. He was tall and handsome, and his eyes were soft as they looked at her. She felt her stomach flip. Maybe . . . maybe it wasn't too late for her after all?

Jeanette rushed into the tent as they came off stage. 'Felicity! Where's my daughter?'

'Mum! You're not meant to be back here!'

'I couldn't wait to see you,' said Jeanette, her words tumbling out of her. 'Oh, Fliss! You were wonderful out there!' She pulled Fliss into her arms, oblivious to the amused looks from the other girls. 'You were amazing! You made me laugh, made me cry – oh goodness, I cried such bucketloads at the end!' She hugged Fliss even tighter. 'I can see how much you love it, my sweet.' She pulled back suddenly to look into Fliss's face. 'I still think acting is an unstable career,' she said seriously, 'but I can see you've got real talent.' She took a breath. 'I'll do what I can to support you if you decide it's really what you want to do.'

'Oh, Mum!' Fliss's face lit up. 'It is, it is! Oh, I'd be so happy if I could act!'

Candy, coming into the tent, overheard this and laughed. 'You're already on your way,' she said. 'Jeanette, you've got a very talented daughter there.'

'I know,' said Jeanette proudly.

Candy hesitated. 'Fliss, I might as well tell you now. There was a friend of mine in to watch the show this afternoon. He's a TV producer. He wants you to audition for a new series he's working on.'

The whole tent fell silent for a moment, and then there was an outburst of whooping and cheering. 'Fliss is going to be on TV!' yelled Mari, grabbing Victoria and jumping up and down. 'Our little Fliss!'

Candy laughed again. 'Well, not yet. But maybe. He was very impressed with you,' she said softly to Fliss. 'You did well. That's the best I've seen you perform.'

Fliss could hardly speak, she felt so happy. But she felt she needed to explain something to Candy. 'I can't really remember the play,' she said in a low voice. 'I mean, I can't remember performing it. I was just in another world the whole time.'

Candy smiled. 'I know. That's what marks you out as such a good actor.'

'Come on,' said Jeanette, who was still looking

stunned at Candy's news. 'Get out of your costume and we'll go have a celebratory supper.'

'I will,' said Fliss, suddenly remembering something, 'but can I meet you out the front? I need to do something before we go.'

Jeanette lifted her eyebrows knowingly. 'Something to do with that handsome young Romeo, I expect?'

Fliss blushed, aware that Mari and Victoria were pretending not to listen. 'Yes. I need to tell him something. Then I'll come straight back out, I promise.'

'I'll look after your mum.' Candy took Jeanette's arm. 'Let me talk to you about drama school,' they heard her say as she left the tent.

Mari gripped Fliss's arm so tightly she yelped. 'TV! Fliss, do you know what this means? This could be your big break! You could be famous!'

'Get off me,' Fliss laughed, pulling her arm away. 'I've got to pass an audition first, Mari.'

Mari flapped her hand as though that wasn't important. 'Yes, yes, but when you pass it – the world is your lobster!'

'Oyster,' said Victoria.

'What?'

'The world is your oyster. That's the phrase.'

Mari looked taken aback. 'Is it? I'm sure it's lobster, my mum always says lobster.'

Fliss slipped out of her costume while the other two were arguing. She felt almost unreal, as though all these amazing things were happening to someone else. Maybe she was still playing Juliet, and none of this was real? She took a quick glance in her hand mirror before grabbing her bag and leaving the tent quietly. Mari and Victoria were still arguing. Fliss grinned. She'd see them later – or tomorrow maybe. But now there was something she had to do.

Tom wasn't in the boys' tent, and for a dreadful moment Fliss thought he had already gone home. But then Sean looked up and saw her. 'Looking for Tom?' he asked.

Fliss blushed. 'Yes. Has he gone?'

Sean shook his head. 'He's helping bring props back from the stage so they can be stored here overnight.'

'Oh, thanks.'

'Good luck,' Sean called after her, but Fliss pretended she hadn't heard. How did Sean know? Had he been talking to Mari?

She heard Tom before she saw him. There was a sudden clatter from behind a bush and some rude words. 'Tom?' Fliss rounded the bush and saw that

Tom had been carrying the swords and dropped them on his own foot. 'You OK?'

He looked up, rubbing his foot. 'Yeah. Just tripped over something and lost my grip.'

Fliss helped him pick them up again. 'Um, Tom?'

He started off down the path again. 'Yeah?'

She hurried after him. 'Can we . . . I need to talk to you.'

'OK, well, I've sort of got my hands full at the moment.' Tom reached the boys' tent and passed the swords to Sean.

'Oh, Fliss was looking for you,' said Sean. Then he caught sight of her. 'Ah.'

Tom turned to face Fliss. 'So – uh . . . what did you want to talk about?'

Fliss was uncomfortably aware of Sean listening inside the tent, and there were several other boys trying not to look interested too. Doug waggled his glasses at her. 'Can we – go somewhere else?'

Tom glanced back into the tent. 'I guess so. Where?'

'Um.' Suddenly Fliss knew exactly where she wanted to go. Surprising herself, she moved forward to take Tom's hand. 'Come with me.'

Her heart thumping in her chest, Fliss led Tom out of the wooded area, across the clearing and up into the bandstand. The afternoon sun was losing its warmth and people were heading home. The bandstand was empty.

Tom looked puzzled. 'Here?'

Fliss faced him. 'Here.' She took a breath. 'I've got some things to say and I want you to just listen until I've finished, OK?'

Tom nodded, his eyes fixed on hers.

Fliss took another breath. *You can do this*, she told herself. *You faced Samantha. In front of everyone. You can surely tell Tom how you feel about him.* But this was a lot scarier than the confrontation with Samantha. She twisted her fingers together to try to give herself strength. 'I have to tell you . . .' she began, but that didn't sound right. 'I wanted to say . . .' That wasn't right either.

Tom said nothing, but his gaze seemed to go right through her. Looking into his eyes, those deep blue pools, seemed to give Fliss the courage she needed.

'Ages ago,' she said, 'you asked me to go for a burger or something with you. I turned you down.' Tom opened his mouth, but Fliss hurried on. 'No, don't say anything. I turned you down because I was scared. I didn't know how to be with you; how to even talk to you. I only felt confident when I was in character – playing a role. And when you started going out with

Samantha, I thought I'd blown it. I thought you'd gone off me. But then there was that thunderstorm . . .' Fliss's voice faltered, and she cleared her throat. 'The thunderstorm,' she said more firmly. 'And you – you were going to kiss me. And I really wanted you to.' She looked earnestly at him. '*Really* wanted you to. But all the time, I knew you were going out with Samantha. And that made me scared again. I thought you were just messing around. To be honest, I didn't know *what* was going on. But I was too scared to take that step – to risk it. And you already had a girlfriend! So I couldn't do anything.'

'Fliss . . .'

'No, I haven't finished.' Fliss's voice was beginning to shake again, and she knew she was coming up to the hardest part. 'I don't know why you went out with Samantha. I don't want to know. But now you're not . . . and what I wanted to say was . . . I really like you.' She glanced up into his eyes again. 'I can't stop thinking about you. All those rehearsals we had together – I looked forward to them because I was going to see you. And I still feel that way. So . . .' Here it came. 'So if you want to . . . I'd really like to go get that burger sometime. If you want.'

There was a long silence after Fliss had finished. She felt as though something heavy had been lifted from her shoulders. She had said it! And it hadn't been the end of the world!

But what would Tom say?

He stared at her for a long moment, and then he smiled. It was the most beautiful smile in the world to Fliss. She felt the corners of her own mouth curl up in response. And then he was laughing and shaking his head, as if he couldn't believe what he'd just heard. Fliss felt a quiver of fear. Did he think she was joking?

'You,' he said. 'What are you like? I thought you were this little mouse – and now it turns out you're a lion!'

Fliss smiled uncertainly. 'Is that good?'

He reached out to touch her face and his eyes softened. 'It's very good,' he said gently. 'You're so amazing. I thought you were amazing at our first rehearsal. But you always seemed so quiet. I couldn't tell what you were thinking. I thought you weren't interested.'

'I was, I was,' whispered Fliss, mesmerized.

'But you didn't say anything.' Tom sighed. 'I never asked Samantha out, you know. It just happened somehow, and I wasn't strong enough to say no. And I thought you didn't care . . .' His hand stroked her hair. 'But now I know you do . . .'

His face was inches away. 'Yes?' breathed Fliss. She couldn't move.

'I can see why you wanted to talk here,' said Tom softly. 'It's the perfect place, isn't it? No more playing a character. No more pretending to be someone else. Just you – and me.' He bent his head to hers, and Fliss thought she might faint from the overwhelming feeling that was sweeping from her toes up to the top of her head.

'Fliss! Fliss! Where are you?'

It was Jeanette's voice. Tom paused. He was so close Fliss could feel his breath on her cheek. He smiled and said, 'Looks like we're being interrupted again.'

'I don't care,' Fliss whispered back. She had waited so long for this moment, she wasn't going to let anyone take it from her! Without even thinking, she reached out and cupped Tom's face with both hands. Then she kissed him on the lips.

It was only a short kiss but it felt like it lasted for hours. Tom's lips were soft and warm and Fliss thought for a second that her feet had left the ground. Nothing existed around her. It was only Tom – Tom and nothing and nobody else.

When she pulled back, Fliss was smiling. Tom looked dazed. 'You are the same Fliss, right?' he said in a shaky voice.

She nodded. 'A sort of new and improved version, maybe.'

'Wow.'

'Yeah. Yes, I think so.' She grinned at him. 'So, call me, OK? And we'll go out for that burger. Right?'

'Right.' He grinned back. 'I guess you're in charge. And, can I just say again – wow. I'm going to like getting to know the new you.'

Fliss shook her head. 'It's the same as the old me. With a bit more confidence, that's all.'

'I like it.'

'See you then.' Fliss jumped the last few steps to the grass, leaving Tom standing in the middle of the bandstand, his curly hair ruffled and his deep blue eyes never leaving her. She picked up her bag and started across the park. The smile spread across her face, wider and wider, as she thought about all the incredible things that had only happened in the last day. The memories fizzed up inside her like fireworks and suddenly Fliss exploded into laughter.

Fliss ran across the grass, faster and faster, as the light faded from the sky and the stars came out.

You can meet some of the **Star Crossed**
girls again in the brand-new

book

Strictly Friends?

Available September 2010

Read on for a special look . . .

The door burst open and in came a rather dishevelled-looking girl with thick blonde hair scooped into an untidy ponytail. She looked around. 'Really sorry I'm late. It – er – my mum . . . well, never mind.' She dumped her jacket and bag on the floor and made an exclamation of annoyance. 'Oh, no! Sorry, I seem to have walked half the field in on my shoes.' There was indeed a trail of muddy footprints leading from the door. 'I'll take them off,' she said, wrestling with her trainers without undoing the laces.

Megan wanted to laugh. The girl seemed completely oblivious to the fact she'd just interrupted everything. Some of the other girls were glaring at her, but Megan had to hide her smile. The blonde girl looked up and caught Megan's eye. She grinned back. 'Nearly done.'

Corinne was looking amused too. 'When you've quite finished . . .' She frowned for a moment. 'Don't I know you?'

The girl nodded. 'From *Romeo and Juliet*. I was the Nurse.'

'Ah, that's right,' said Corinne. 'Mari, isn't it? Talked through most of those rehearsals too, didn't you?'

'Not *all* of them,' said Mari, grinning.

'Right,' said Corinne. 'Shall we get started?'

Mari came to stand by Megan. 'I see you came with the right shoes,' she said, glancing at Megan's black jazz shoes. 'I'm just going to have to dance in socks.'

'That's all right,' said Megan. 'It won't matter.'

Corinne began explaining the basic salsa step, and Megan looked around the room. There were about twelve of them, she guessed, and all girls, of course. Megan had hardly been expecting anything else, but she felt a bit disappointed nonetheless. This wouldn't be a good class for her. She was way beyond the basics, and she needed a partner to dance with if she wanted to carry on training. Megan wondered just how far away she would need to travel to find one.

To her left, Mari was stomping around in an attempt to follow Corinne. 'This is ridiculous,' she muttered. 'I've got no sense of rhythm.'

Megan laughed. 'I'm guessing it wasn't your idea to come tonight?'

'You're so right,' said Mari with feeling. 'My mother thinks I need to lose some weight. She drew up a long list of things she wanted me to join, but I put my foot down. I mean – *hockey* club?' She shuddered. 'I tried badminton last term but I have no hand–eye co-ordination and I was just rubbish. This was the only other activity on the list that took place indoors.'

Megan grinned. 'Is that why you said you were only coming for one lesson?'

The expression on Mari's face was comical. 'You heard that? Oh, no, how embarrassing. I don't want Corinne to think I've come along to mess about.' She tried the step again. 'My legs just won't do that.'

'Here.' Megan took up position beside her. 'It's quite simple really. Step forward-back-close. Then back-forward-close. That's it.'

'That's it?' Mari looked surprised. 'Doesn't seem like much.'

'It isn't, but the whole dance is based on that basic step.' Megan demonstrated. 'And it's all about timing. One, two three . . . five, six, seven. Like this.'

'Wow,' said Mari. 'You look like you've done it before.'

'I have,' admitted Megan. 'I've been ballroom dancing since I was six.'

'Six!' exclaimed Mari. 'The only thing I've been doing since I was six is eating.' She pulled a face. 'As my mother keeps pointing out.'

Megan hesitated. 'You don't look fat to me.'

'You're sweet. I don't look fat to me either, but Mum keeps measuring my body mass index and pointing out I'm verging on obese. Nice.'

'OK!' called Corinne. 'Everyone got that step now? Good. The salsa isn't just about the steps though. It's about attitude. You've got to swing your hips . . .'

Megan enjoyed the rest of the class, mostly because of Mari, who made her laugh. There were other girls in the class who were quick to pick up the steps, and it was clear many of them had done some kind of dance before. At least they hadn't spent the whole hour just doing the basic step over and over again, reflected Megan as she changed her shoes. They had learned enough for Corinne to put together a simple routine.

'Please say you'll be my partner again next week,' Mari begged as she pulled on her outdoor shoes. 'I might stand a chance of remembering it then.'

'I thought you weren't coming back next week,' said Megan, amused. 'You said you would only come for one lesson.'

Mari went slightly pink. 'Well, it wasn't as bad as I thought,' she said. 'I did think maybe the class would be full of stuck-up ballerinas.'

Megan let out a snort of laughter. 'Don't say that too loudly. Nothing wrong with ballet.'

'Indeed not,' said Corinne, who had overheard this. 'Ballet gives you grace and strength, Mari.' She looked at her pointedly. 'Maybe it would be good for you.'

'I am *not* doing ballet,' said Mari positively. Her expression softened. 'But this was OK. I think I could do this.'

Corinne turned to Megan. 'You've done salsa before, I could tell. Have you been to ballroom lessons somewhere else?'

Megan nodded. 'We only just moved to the area last week. I'm from Yorkshire. I started ballroom when I was six.'

Corinne looked sympathetic. 'This class will probably be a bit frustrating for you.'

'I sort of thought maybe you'd know if there were other classes I could go to,' said Megan hesitantly.

Corinne looked thoughtful, but then she shook her head. 'Not that I can think of,' she said. 'This isn't a very dance-orientated town, as you may have guessed. I mean, there's ballet and tap and jazz. But not ballroom. It's still a bit of a speciality.'

'That's what I thought,' said Megan, though her heart sank. 'Never mind. I quite enjoyed this evening.'

'Maybe there's something we can do to use your

skills a bit more,' said Corinne. 'Leave it with me. I'll think of something.'

The other girls were leaving. Mari looked at Megan. 'So, are *you* coming next week then?'

Megan smiled at her. 'I guess so. At least for the moment.' She glanced up and noticed the clock. It was ten past seven already! 'Oh, no! I should be home by now! My mum will be sending out a search party.' She grabbed her bag hastily. 'Thanks, Corinne. See you next week.'

It was still light outside, but Megan knew her mother would be anxiously standing by the window, waiting for her to come home. And after she'd promised to be back by five past seven too! She hoped Mum wouldn't be bundling Owen's coat over his pyjamas as she promised. Megan raced round the corner to the skate park.

'*Oof!*'

'Oh God – I'm so sorry!' Megan looked down at the boy lying on the ground. 'I completely didn't see you! Here . . .' She offered him a hand, but the boy pulled himself up, panting.

'Are you blind?' he exclaimed, brushing down his jeans.

Megan felt embarrassed. 'No. I'm sorry, I was in a hurry. Are you all right?'

The boy looked at her. He was taller than Megan, with jet-black hair that looked like it might be dyed. His eyes were a sharp, icy blue, and his face – well. Megan gulped. This boy was quite possibly the most good-looking boy she had ever seen. He had high, defined cheekbones and dark eyelashes and eyebrows. He looked like a model.

'Who are you?' he demanded. 'Are you new around here?'

'Yes,' said Megan, but her voice was croaky and she had to clear her throat. 'Yes,' she said again. 'Just moved in round the corner.'

The boy looked at her searchingly, taking in her shoulder-length auburn hair, her green eyes and her slim figure. He nodded slowly, and a strange expression crossed his face. He seemed about to say something but then changed his mind. Instead, he nodded once more, and said, 'Well, see you.' Then he bent to pick up a skateboard that up to now Megan hadn't even noticed. With a swift movement, the boy stepped onto it and pushed off. They were at the top of a slight slope, and the board quickly picked up speed. Megan watched as he skimmed over a ramp and up another slope. There were a couple of others watching too, but Megan only had time to notice they were two girls and a boy before a voice behind her made her jump.

'Megan! Thank goodness! What are you *doing?*'

Megan turned to see Nicola hurrying up, Owen in his pyjamas and clutching his leopard in her arms. Owen was protesting loudly.

'Mum! I'm so sorry, it's only ten past, isn't it?'

'Fifteen minutes past,' said Nicola in an acid tone. 'And now I find out you've been standing around chatting.'

'I haven't, honestly.' Megan followed Nicola home, trying to explain about crashing into the boy and having to stop to apologize.

'Well,' said Nicola, as they arrived at the front door, 'one thing's for certain. You won't be walking home alone again.'

Megan bit her lip. If she wasn't going to be allowed to walk home on her own, how on earth would she ever get to talk to that boy again? Because she suddenly realized she really, really wanted to.